Ragnarok

Also by A.S. Byatt

Fiction

The Shadow of the Sun
The Game
The Virgin in the Garden
Still Life
Sugar and Other Stories
Possession: A Romance
Angels and Insects
The Matisse Stories
The Djinn in the Nightingale's Eye
Babel Tower
Elementals
The Biographer's Tale
A Whistling Woman
Little Black Book of Stories
The Children's Book

Criticism

Degrees of Freedom: The Novels of Iris Murdoch
Unruly Times: Wordsworth and Coleridge in their Time
Passions of the Mind: Selected Writings
Imagining Characters (with Ignês Sodré)
On Histories and Stories: Selected Essays
Portraits in Fiction
Memory: An Anthology (edited with Harriet Harvey Wood)

Ragnarok

The End of the Gods

A.S. BYATT

CANONGATE
Edinburgh · London

This edition first published in 2012 by Canongate Books

First published in Great Britain in 2011 by Canongate Books Ltd,
14 High Street, Edinburgh EH1 1TE

1

British Library Cataloguing-in-Publication Data
A catalogue record for this book is available on
request from the British Library

ISBN 978 1 84767 297 1
Export ISBN 978 1 84767 935 2

Typeset in Van Dijck by Palimpsest Book Production Ltd,
Falkirk, Stirlingshire

Printed and bound in Great Britain by
Clays Ltd, St Ives plc

www.canongate.tv

For my mother,

K.M. Drabble,

Who gave me *Asgard and the Gods*.

A Note on Names

This story has been made from many stories in many languages – Icelandic, German and others. The names of the persons in the myth vary from telling to telling. Iduna is the same person as Idun. There are many ways of spelling Jørmungandr or Jörmungander. I feel happier using various spellings, rather than trying to achieve an artificial consistency. Myths change in the mind depending on the telling – there is no overall correct version.

WODAN'S WILD HUNT

A THIN CHILD IN WARTIME

There was a thin child, who was three years old when the world war began. She could remember, though barely, the time before wartime when, as her mother frequently told her, there was honey and cream and eggs in plenty. She was a thin, sickly, bony child, like an eft, with fine hair like sunlit smoke. Her elders told her not to do this, to avoid that, because there was 'a war on'. Life was a state in which a war was on. Nevertheless, by a paradoxical fate, the child may only have lived because her people left the sulphurous air of a steel city, full of smoking chimneys, for a country town, of no interest to enemy bombers. She grew up in the ordinary paradise of the English countryside. When she was five she walked to school, two miles, across meadows covered with cowslips, buttercups, daisies, vetch, rimmed by hedges full of blossom and then berries, blackthorn, hawthorn, dog-roses, the odd ash tree with its sooty buds.

Her mother, when they appeared, always said 'black as ash-buds in the front of March'. Her mother's fate too was paradoxical. Because there was a war on, it was legally possible for her to live in the mind, to teach bright boys, which before the war had been forbidden to married women. The thin child learned to read very early. Her mother was more real, and kinder, when it was a question of grouped letters on the page. Her father was away. He was in the air, in the war, in Africa, in Greece, in Rome, in a world that only existed in books. She remembered him. He had red-gold hair and clear blue eyes, like a god.

The thin child knew, and did not know that she knew, that her elders lived in provisional fear of imminent destruction. They faced the end of the world they knew. The English country world did not end, as many others did, was not overrun, nor battered into mud by armies. But fear was steady, even if no one talked to the thin child about it. In her soul she knew her bright father would not come back. At the end of every year the family sipped cider and toasted his safe return. The thin child felt a despair she did not know she felt.

THE ASH, YGGDRASIL

THE END OF THE WORLD

The Beginning

The thin child thought less (or so it now seems) of where she herself came from, and more about that old question, why is there something rather than nothing? She devoured stories with rapacious greed, ranks of black marks on white, sorting themselves into mountains and trees, stars, moons and suns, dragons, dwarfs, and forests containing wolves, foxes and the dark. She told her own tales as she walked through the fields, tales of wild riders and deep meres, of kindly creatures and evil hags.

At some point, when she was a little older, she discovered *Asgard and the Gods*. This was a solid volume, bound in green, with an intriguing, rushing image on the cover, of Odin's Wild Hunt on horseback tearing through a clouded sky amid jagged bolts of lightning, watched, from the entrance to a dark underground cavern, by a dwarf in a cap, looking alarmed. The book was full of immensely detailed, mysterious steel engravings of wolves and wild waters, apparitions and floating women. It was an academic book, and had in fact been used by her mother as a crib for exams in Old Icelandic and Ancient Norse. It was, however, German. It was adapted from the work of Dr W. Wägner. The thin child was given to reading books from cover to cover. She read the introduction, about the retrieval of 'the old Germanic world, with its secrets and wonders . . .' She was puzzled by the idea of the Germans. She had dreams that there were Germans under her bed, who, having cast her parents into a green pit in a dark wood, were sawing down the legs of her bed to reach her and destroy her. Who were these old Germans, as opposed to the ones overhead, now dealing death out of the night sky?

The book also said that these stories belonged to 'Nordic' peoples, Norwegians, Danes and Icelanders. The thin child was, in England, a northerner. The family came from land invaded and settled by Vikings. These were her stories. The book became a passion.

Much of her reading was done late at night,

with a concealed torch under the bedclothes, or with the volume pushed past a slit-opening of the bedroom door into a pool of bleak light on the blacked-out landing. The other book she read and reread, repeatedly, was John Bunyan's *Pilgrim's Progress*. She felt in her bones the crippling burden born by the Man mired in the Slough of Despond, she followed his travels through wilderness and the Valley of the Shadow, his encounters with Giant Despair and the fiend Apollyon. Bunyan's tale had a clear message and meaning. Not so, *Asgard and the Gods*. That book was an account of a mystery, of how a world came together, was filled with magical and powerful beings, and then came to an end. A real End. The end.

One of the illustrations showed Rocks in the Riesengebirge. A river ran through a cleft, above which towered tall lumps of rock with featureless almost-heads, and stumps of almost-arms, standing amongst thrusting columns with no resemblance to any living form. Grey spiked forest tips clothed one slope. Tiny, ant-like, almost invisible humans stared upwards from the near shore. Wraiths of cloud-veils hung between the forms and the reading child. She read:

The legends of the giants and dragons were developed gradually, like all myths. At first natural objects were looked upon as identical with these strange beings, then the rocks and chasms became their dwelling-places, and finally they were regarded as distinct personalities and had their own kingdom of Jotunheim.

The picture gave the child an intense, uncanny pleasure. She knew, but could not have said, that it was the precise degree of formlessness in the nevertheless scrupulously depicted rocks that was so satisfactory. The reading eye must do the work to make them live, and so it did, again and again, never the same life twice, as the artist had intended. She had noticed that a bush, or a log, seen from a distance on her meadow-walk, could briefly be a crouching, snarling dog, or a trailing branch could be a snake, complete with shining eyes and flickering forked tongue.

This way of looking was where the gods and giants came from.

The stone giants made her want to write.

They filled the world with alarming energy and power.

She saw their unformed faces, peering at herself from behind the snout of her gas-mask, during air-raid drill.

Every Wednesday the elementary-school children went to the local church for scripture lessons. The vicar was kindly: light came through a coloured window above his head.

There were pictures and songs of gentle Jesus meek and mild. In one of them he preached in a clearing to a congregation of attentive cuddly animals, rabbits, a fawn, a squirrel, a magpie. The animals were more real than the divine-human figure. The thin child tried to respond to the picture, and failed.

They were taught to say prayers. The thin child had an intuition of wickedness as she felt what she spoke sucked into a cotton-wool cloud of nothingness.

She was a logical child, as children go. She did not understand how such a nice, kind, good God as the one they prayed to, could condemn the whole earth for sinfulness and flood it, or condemn his only Son to a disgusting death on behalf of everyone. This death did not seem to have done much good. There was a war on. Possibly there would always be a war on. The fighters on the other side were bad and not saved, or possibly were human and hurt.

The thin child thought that these stories – the sweet, cotton-wool meek and mild one, the barbaric sacrificial gloating one, were both human make-ups, like the life of the giants in the Riesengebirge. Neither aspect made her want to write, or fed her imagination. They numbed it. She tried to think she might be wicked for thinking these things. She might be like Ignorance, in *Pilgrim's Progress*, who fell into the pit at the gate of heaven. She tried to feel wicked.

But her mind veered away, to where it was alive.

Yggdrasil: the World-Ash

I know an ash, it is called Yggdrasil
A hairy tree, moistened by a brilliant cloud.

In the beginning was the tree. The stone ball rushed through emptiness. Under the crust was fire. Rocks boiled, gases seethed. Blebs burst through the crust. Dense salt water clung to the rolling ball. Slime slid on it and in the slime shapes shifted. Any point on a ball is the centre and the tree was at the centre. It held the world together, in the air, in the earth, in the light, in the dark, in the mind.

It was a huge creature. It pushed root-needles into thick mulch. After the blind tips came threads and ropes and cables, which probed and gripped and searched. Its three roots reached under meadows and mountains, under Midgard, middle earth, out to Jotunheim, home of the ice-giants, down in the dark to the vapours of Hel.

Its tall trunk was compacted of woody rings, one inside the other, pressing outwards. Close inside its skin were tubes in bundles, pulling up unbroken columns of water to the branches and the canopy. The strength of the tree moved the flow of the water, up to the leaves, which opened in the light from the sun, and mixed light, water, air and earth to make new green matter, moving in the wind, sucking in the rain. The green stuff ate light. At night, as light faded, the tree gave it back, shining briefly in twilight like a pale lamp.

The tree ate and was eaten, fed and was fed on. Its vast underearth mesh and highway of roots was infested and swathed by threads of fungus, which fed on the roots, wormed their way into the cells themselves and sucked out life. Only occasionally did these thriving thread-creatures push up through the forest floor, or through the bark, to make mush-rooms or toadstools, scarlet and leathery, with white warts, pale-skinned fragile umbrellas, woody layered protrusions on the bark itself. Or they rose on their own stalks and made puffballs, which burst and spread spores like smoke. They fed on the tree but they also carried food to the tree, fine fragments to be raised in the pillar of water.

There were worms, fat as fingers, fine as hairs, pushing blunt snouts through the mulch, eating roots, excreting root food. Beetles were busy in the bark, gnashing and piercing, breeding and feeding, shining like metals, brown like dead wood. Woodpeckers drilled the bark, and ate fat grubs who ate the tree. They flashed in the branches, green and crimson, black, white and scarlet. Spiders hung on silk, attached fine-woven webs to leaves and twigs, hunted bugs, butterflies, soft moths, strutting crickets. Ants swarmed up in frenzied armies, or farmed sweet aphids, stroked with fine feelers. Pools formed in the pits where the branches forked; moss sprouted; bright tree-frogs swam in the pools, laid delicate eggs and gulped in jerking and spiralling wormlings. Birds sang at the twigs' ends and built nests of all kinds – clay cup, hairy bag, soft hay-lined bowl, hidden in holes in the bark. All over its surface the tree was scraped and scavenged, bored and gnawed, minced and mashed.

Tales were told of other creatures in the society amongst the spreading branches. At their crown, it seemed, stood an eagle, singing indifferently of past, present and what was to come. Its name was Hraesvelgr, 'flesh-swallower'; when its wings beat, winds blew, tempests howled. Between the eyes of the huge bird stood a fine falcon, Vedrfölnir. The great branches were pasture for grazing creatures, four stags, Daínn, Dvalinn, Dúneyrr and Duraþrór, and a goat, Heidrún, whose udder was filled with honey-mead. A busy black squirrel, 'drill-tooth', Ratatöskr, scurried busily from summit to root and back, carrying malicious messages from the bird on the crown to the watchful black dragon, curled around the roots, Nidhøggr, entwined with a brood of coiling worms. Nidhøggr gnawed the roots, which renewed themselves.

The tree was immense. It supported, or shaded, high halls and palaces. It was a world in itself.

At its foot was a black, measureless well, whose dark waters, when drunk, gave wisdom, or at least insight. At its rim sat the Fatal Sisters, the Norns, who may have come from Jotunheim. Urd saw the past, Werdandi saw the present and Skuld stared into the future. The well too was called Urd. The sisters were spinners, who twisted the threads of fate. They were the gardeners and guardians of the Tree. They watered the tree with the black well-water. They fed it with pure white clay, *aurr*. So it decayed, or was diminished, from moment to moment. So it was always renewed.

Rándrasill

In the kelp forests grew a monstrous bull-kelp, Rándrasill, the Sea-Tree. It gripped the underwater rock with a tough holdfast, from which rose the stem like a whiplash taller than the masts or rooftrees, the stipe. The stipe went up and up from the depths to the surface, glassy still, whipped by winds, swaying lazy. Where the water met the air the stipe spread into thickets of fronds and streamers, each buoyed up by a pocket of gas, a bladder at its base. The branching fronds, like those of the Tree on land, were threaded with green cells that ate light. Seawater takes in red light; floating dust and debris take in blue; weeds deep down in dim light are mostly red in colour, whereas those tossing on the surface, or clinging to tide-washed ledges, can be brilliant green or glistening yellow. The sea-tree grew at great speed. Strips tore away and new ones sprouted, new weed-spawn streamed from the fronds in milky clouds, or green clouds, of moving creatures that swam free before gripping at rock. In the water-forest creatures ate and were eaten, as they were in the roots and branches of the land-tree.

The tree was grazed by wandering snails and sea-slugs, rasping up specks of life, animal, vegetable. Filter-feeding sponges sucked at the thicket of stipes; sea-anemones clung to the clinging weed, and opened and closed their fringed, fleshy mouths. Horn-coated, clawed creatures, shrimp and spiny lobster, brittle-stars and featherstars supped. Spiny urchin-balls roamed and chewed. There were multitudes of crabs: porcelain crabs, great spider crabs, scorpion and spiky stone crabs, masked crabs, circular crabs, edible crabs, harbour crabs, swimming crabs, angular crabs, each with its own roaming-ground. There were sea-cucumbers, amphipods, mussels, barnacles, tunicates and polychaete worms. All ate the wood and fed the weed with their droppings and decay.

Things swayed, and slid, and sailed through the sea-forest, hunting and hunted. Some were fish-flesh disguised as weeds – angler-fish enveloped in floating veils like sargassum, dragon-fish hanging in the water indistinguishable from frond-forms, draped in shawls and banners like tattered vegetable protrusions. And there were huge fish with bladed bodies, refracting light, lurking shadows in the shadows, their swaying flanks changing colour as the light streamed through the water and was sifted.

The Sea-Tree stood in a world of other sea-growth, from the vast tracts of bladderwrack to the sea-tangles, tangleweeds, oarweeds, seagirdles, horsetail kelps, devil's aprons and mermaid's wine-glasses. Shoals of great fish and small fish went by, wheeling packed globes of herring, rushing herds of tunny. There were salmon on their long journeys – chinook, coho, sockeye, pink, chum and cherry salmon. There were green turtles grazing in the fronds. There were streamlined sharks in many forms, thresher, shortfin mako, porbeagle, tope, leopard shark, dusky shark, sandbar shark and night shark, the hunters of the hunters of the hunted. Great whales tore giant squid from the depths, or opened the vast sieves of their mouths to filter plankton. Creatures built homes in the canopy as creatures built homes in the World-Ash. Sea otters constructed cradles and dangled from the fronds, turning shellfish and urchins in busy forepaws. Dolphins danced and sang, clicking and whistling. Seabirds screamed overhead and plumped like arrows into the mass of water. The water was pulled this way and that by the sun and the moon. Tides crawled up beaches, were sucked into inlets, broke with white lacy spray on shells of rock, hurtled in smooth and rearing, or seeped and meandered in deltas.

The holdfast of the Sea-Tree was on an underwater mountainside, deep, deep down, as far as the last glimmer of sunlight or moonlight could penetrate. There were deeper things. There were creatures of the dark whose plated forms, or spiny or fleshy heads, were lit as though by brilliant lamps in the black gloom. Things that angled for prey with a fishing line of their own flesh, things whose eyes glared in the visible darkness.

At the foot of the World-Ash is the Fountain of Urd: still, cold, black water. At the foot of the Sea-Tree are vents and funnels, through which whistle steam, and spittings of molten stone from the hot centre of the earth. Here too, in darkness, worms crawl, and pallid prawns flicker glassy feelers. As the three women from Jotunheim, the Norns, sit at the edge of the fountain and feed and water the Tree, so Aegir and Rán sit in the currents that eddy about the holdfast of Rándrasill. Aegir makes music with a stringed harp and a pearly conch. Whales and dolphins hang motionless, sifting the singing through the echo-chambers of their heads. The sounds can act like oil on the ocean, making a dull calm, or a glistening calm, seen glassy from under, and sparking from above. There are other tunes which perturb currents, and send great tongues of water bellowing up, as high above the thin surface as the tree is above the holdfast. The mass of water, glassy green, basalt black, holds for an everlasting moment and then the crest crumbles down and drives deep again, shedding foam, and froth, and billions of bubbles of air. Aegir's wife, Rán, plays with a vast net which she loops about dead and dying creatures as they fall through the thick depths. Some say things are caught in her toils that are neither dead nor dying, but only entranced by the welling sound. What she does with the bones and baleen, the skin and scrags, is not known. It is said that she plants them in sand, to feed what crawls and creeps under it. It is said that she collects the very beautiful – a luminous squid, a sailor with thick gold hair, blue eyes and a lapis earring, an errant sea-snake – and arranges them in a weed-garden, for the pleasure of staring. Those who see her see nothing else, and do not return to describe her.

Homo Homini Deus Est

The thin child in wartime considered the question of how something came out of nothing. In the story told in the stone church a grandfatherly figure who resented presumption had spent six delectable days making things – sky and sea, sun and moon, the trees and the seaweeds, the camel, the horse, the peacock, the dog, the cat, the worm, all creatures that on earth do dwell to sing to him with cheerful voices, to sing his praises that was, as the angels incessantly did. And he had put the humans in their place and had told them to keep their place and not to eat the knowledge of good and evil. The thin child knew enough fairy stories to know that a prohibition in a story is only there to be broken. The first humans were fated to eat the apple. The dice were loaded against them. The grandfather was pleased with himself. The thin child found no one in this story with whom to sympathise.

Except maybe the snake, which had not asked to be made use of as a tempter. The snake wanted simply to coil about in the branches.

What was there in the beginning in the Asgard stories?

> In the first age
> There was nothing
> Nor sand nor sea
> Nor cold waves;
> There was no earth,
> No sky on high.
> The gulf gaped
> And grass grew nowhere.

The empty gulf had a name, Ginnungagap, which the thin child repeated again and again. It was a wonderful word. It was not entirely formless. It was bounded by points of the compass. To the north was Niflheim, home of mists, the place of cold and wet, from which roared twelve violent streams of icy water. To the south was Muspelheim, the hot place, where fire scorched and smoked. Icebergs rolled from Niflheim and were melted to steam by the hot blast from Muspelheim. In the swirling chaos a human form was shaped from the spitting matter, the giant Ymir, or Aurgelmir, whose name meant seething clay or gravel-yeller. He was made, some said, of the pure white clay with which the Norns fed Yggdrasil. He was vast: he was everything, or almost everything. The thin child saw him spread-eagled, glistening all over, for some reason faceless, his head a rocky globe.

There was another creature in Ginnungagap, a huge cow, constantly making milk as she licked the salt on the ice-rocks. Ymir fed on the milk. The thin child could not imagine how. There was too much of him. He was the father of the Hrimthurses, the frost-giants, who budded from his bulk. In the pit where his left arm met his trunk, creatures formed, male and female; his feet coiled together and gave birth to a male being. Meanwhile the great cow, busily supping the salt with her hot tongue, uncovered, first the curled hair, then the sleeping frost-flesh of another giant, Burr, who gave birth to another, Bor, who found somewhere (where? thought the thin child, her head crammed with giants over-whelming Ginnungagap) a giantess called Bestla, who gave birth to three sons, the first gods, Odin, Wili and We.

These three set upon Ymir, slaughtered him and dismembered him.

The thin child tried to imagine this. It could be contemplated if she reduced everything in size, so that Ginnungagap and its contents resembled a thick glass ball, inside which the mist blew like ropes, and the clay man sprawled in space, glistening with frost. They crept up on him, the first gods, and tore him open – with fingernails, with teeth, with scythes, with hooks, with what? They tore him limb from limb, a phrase she knew well. They did not have faces, they were not persons, these three gods, they moved like running black shadows, like rat-men, stabbing and searching. This first act of the new gods took place in three colours, the first that humans see and name, black, white and red. The Gap was black, many shades of black, thick and fine, glossy and tenebrous. The great snowman was white, except where his own parts cast white-violet shadows, in the pits of his arms, in his monstrous nostrils, under his knees. The new gods hacked and laughed. Blood spurted from the wounds they made, poured from his neck over his shoulders, slid like a hot garment over his chest and flanks, flowed, flowed, filled the glass ball with running crimson, and drowned the world. It was unquenchable, it was the life that had been in him, under the clay and ice, it drained away into death. There was a story in the Asgard book that the thin child did not like, about a giant called Bergelmir who built a boat and survived the deluge, and became the ancestor of the other giants. She did not like the story because the German writer said it was perhaps an echo of the story of Noah and the Flood. She wanted to keep this tale separate.

The gods made the world from the dead giant. The thin child was disturbed at having to imagine this; there was no scale by which she could measure it, although she could grasp the shadowy semblances that linked the bits of dead Human to the creatures and structures in the world.

> From the flesh of Ymir
> The earth was shaped.
> From his bones, the mountains,

The heaven from the skull
Of the giant cold as frost
And from his blood,
The sea.

The lakes were made from his sweat, and the trees from his curling hair. Inside the high cavern of his skull, his brains became the rolling clouds. The stars were perhaps wandering sparks from Muspelheim which the gods trapped and fixed under the skull bone. Or maybe they were lights above the bone, glimpsed through slits and bore-holes made during the murder.

Maggots and worms of all kinds fed on the festering flesh. The gods made these into cave-dwellers, the dwarf people, the slow strong trolls, the dark-elves. They took the thick eyebrows of the corpse and fashioned them into a bushy fence, containing Midgard, the Garden of Middle Earth. At the centre of Midgard they built the home of the gods, Asgard. These gods called themselves Ases, pillars, and Asgard was circled by Midgard, which was circled by the bloody sea, outside which lay Utgard, the Outside, in which terrible things lurked and prowled.

The gods also made the sun and the moon, and with them, time. The earth was a sprouting corpse and the heaven was the bowl of a skull. Sun and Moon also were human in form. The Sun was a shining woman, in a chariot pulled by a horse, Arwaker (early-waker). The Moon was a bright boy, Mani, driving his horse Alswider (all-swift). Mother Night rode a dark horse, Hrimfaxi (frost-mane) and was followed by her son Day on Skinfaxi (shining mane). These figures, alternating dark and light, hurtled in an endless procession below the skull, above the clouds.

There was something strange about these shining and shadowy drivers and riders. Both sun and moon were hotly pursued by wolves, with open jaws, snapping at their heels, loping across emptiness. The story did not mention any creation of wolves; they simply appeared, snarling and dark. They were a part of the rhythm of things. They never rested or tired. The created world was inside the skull, and the wolves in the mind were there from the outset of the heavenly procession.

The gods built Asgard beautifully. They made tools and weapons, gold pots and beakers, for gold was plentiful, gold disks for hurling and carved gold figures to play games of draughts and chess. They had made the dwarves and trolls, the dark elves and the light. It was at this point that, almost casually, to please or amuse themselves, they made human beings.

There were three gods who left Asgard and went walking for pleasure in the green fields of Midgard. The earth was bright with grass and juicy leeks. The three gods were Odin, Hönir and Lodur, who was, the Asgard book explained, possibly the quick Loki in another form. The three gods came to the seashore and found there two lifeless logs, Ask, the ash, and Embla, who might have been an alder, an elm, or the stump of a vine. These things had nothing.

> They had no mind
> They had no sense
> Nor blood nor sound
> Nor lively colours.

The three gods turned them into living beings. Odin gave them minds, Hönir gave them their senses, and Loki the hot gave them blood and colour. So the three killer-gods became the three lifegivers, supposing, the thin child thought, that Wili and We who had disappeared from the story, had simply been replaced by Hönir and Loki. There were always three, it was a rule of stories, both of myths and fairy tales. It was the Rule of Three. In the Christian story the three are the cross grandfather, the tortured good man, and the white bird with beating wings. Here in this account of the world Odin was a maker, and the others too, to make up three.

The thin child imagined the new woodman and new woodwoman. Their skin was sleek, like new bark, their eyes were bright like watchful birds, they moved fingers and toes in slow surprise, like chickens or snakes emerging from eggs, stumbling a little as they learned to walk. They opened their mouths to smile at each other. They had eaten nothing; they were dead vegetable matter; but their mouths full of new strong white teeth included the canine spikes of the meat-eater, the wolf in the head.

No more is known of the joys or fates of Ask and Embla. Like many things in this tale, they hold together for a brief time, and then return to gaping darkness. But Odin, the god, was a mover of the story. Loki too, if the third wandering god was indeed that trickster, as the thin child liked to believe he was, for it strengthened the links of the chain of the tale if he was there at the making of men.

The thin child walked through the fair field in all weathers, her satchel of books and pens, with the gas-mask hanging from it, like Christian's burden when he walked in the fields, reading in his Book. She thought long and hard, as she walked, about the meaning of belief. She did not believe the stories in *Asgard and the Gods*. But they were coiled like smoke in her skull, humming like dark bees in a hive. She read the Greek stories at school, and said to herself that there had once been people who brought 'belief' to these capricious and quarrelsome gods and goddesses, but she herself read them as she read fairy stories. Puss in Boots, Baba Yaga, brownies, pucks and fairies, foolish and dangerous, nymphs, dryads, hydras and the white winged horse, Pegasus, all these offered the pleasure to the mind that the unreal offers when it is briefly more real than the visible world can ever be. But they didn't live in her, and she didn't live in them.

The church had a real wicket-gate, like the one in *Pilgrim's Progress*, where it was written, Knock, and it shall be opened unto you. Through that gate she trotted, put down satchel and mask, and took up the burden of being required to believe what she *could not* believe – and, she knew, deep in the hollows of her head and body, in her wheezing lungs and space behind the eyes, *did not want* to believe. Bunyan would have found some horrible punishment for her, some slippery slide into a cauldron of boiling fat, some clawed fiend who would carry her away over the crowns of the woods.

The vicar talked gently of gentle Jesus and she felt *rude* not to believe him.

What was alive in the clean stony place that smelled of brass polish, wood polish, was the English language. Almighty and most merciful Father; We have erred, and strayed from thy ways like lost sheep. We have followed too much the devices and desires of our own hearts. We have offended against thy holy laws. We have left undone those things which we ought to have done; And we have done those things which we ought not to have done; And there is no health in us. But thou

O Lord, have mercy upon us, miserable offenders. Spare thou them, O God, which confess their faults.

The thin child knew these words by heart. Sometimes she chanted them as she walked along beside the hedgerow, stressing the words for the rhythm, imagining the lost sheep bleating and peering about in a grey field. But the creed she could not say. She believed in neither the Father, nor the Son, nor the Holy Ghost. She tried to say the words and felt like the bad daughter in the fairy tale, whose throat and mouth were full of wriggling frogs and toads.

She made herself a myth of meadows as she hurried to school and loitered in long afternoons on the way back. They sang, in the church, in the school:

> Daisies are our silver,
>   Buttercups our gold:
> This is all the treasure
>   We can have or hold.
>
> Raindrops are our diamonds
>   And the morning dew;
> While for shining sapphires
>   We've the speedwell blue.

She liked seeing, and learning, and naming things. Daisies. Day's eyes, she learned with a frisson of pleasure. Buttercups, glossy yellow, a lovelier colour than gold, and the ubiquitous dandelions, fiercely yellow with toothed leaves and seedheads finer than wool, their seeds black dots like the tadpoles in the clouds of jelly-spheres in the pond. In spring the field was thick with cowslips, and in the hedgerows, in the tangled bank, under the hawthorn hedge and the ash tree, there were pale primroses and violets of many colours, from rich purple to a white touched with mauve. Dandelion, dent-de-lion, lionstooth, her mother told her. Her mother liked words. There were vetches and lady's bedstraw, forgetmenots and speedwells, foxgloves, viper's bugloss, cow parsley, deadly nightshade (wreathed in the hedges), willowherb and cranesbill, hairy bitter-cress, docks (good for wounds and stings), celan-dines, campions and ragged robin. She watched each one, as they came out, in clumps sprinkled across the grass, or singletons hidden in ditches or attached to stones.

The tangled bank was full of life, most of it unseen, though it could be heard, rustling in dead leaves, or listening to the child listening. You could hear the attention of a hidden bird, or a crouching vole. She watched the spiders weave their perfect geometrical traps, or lurk under an inviting thick silk funnel. There were, at different times of the year, clouds of butterflies, yellow and white, blue, orange and velvet black. The fields were full of sipping, humming bees. The branches and the sky were inhabited by birds. The skylark went up and up out of the bare earth into the blue sky, singing. Thrushes banged snails against stones and left a crackling carpet of empty shells. Rooks strode and cawed and gathered in glossy parliaments in the tree-tops. Huge clouds of starlings went overhead wheeling like one black wing, coiling like smoke. Plovers called.

The thin child fished in the pond for tadpoles and tiddlers, of which there was an endless multitude. She gathered great bunches of wild flowers, cowslips full of honey, scabious in blue cushions, dog-roses, and took them home, where they did not live long, which did not concern her, for there were always more springing up in their place. They flourished and faded and died and always came back next spring, and always would, the thin child thought, long after she herself was dead. Maybe most of all she loved the wild poppies, which made the green bank scarlet as blood. She liked to pick a bud that was fat and ready to open, green-lipped and hairy. Then with her fingers she would prise the petal-case apart, and extract the red, crumpled silk – slightly damp, she thought – and spread it out in the sunlight. She knew in her heart she should not do this. She was cutting a life short, interrupting a natural unfolding, for the pleasure of satisfied curiosity and the glimpse of the secret, scarlet, creased and frilly flower-flesh. Which wilted almost immediately between finger and thumb. But there were always more, so many more. It was all one thing, the field, the hedge, the ash tree, the tangled bank, the trodden path, the innumerable forms of life, of which the thin child, having put down her bundle and gas-mask, was only one among many.

Asgard

The gods in Asgard feasted and drank mead from golden plates and golden cups. They delighted in metalwork, most particularly in gold, and acquired hoards of trinkets and magic rings from the dark smithies of the dwarves. They played practical jokes on each other, and quarrelled. They went to the edge of the circle of Midgard and confronted giants, came back and sang their own praises. The thin child formed the view that both the Christian heaven and the Nordic one were boring, possibly because mortal men could not understand them. There were the saints, in the hymn they sang, casting down their golden crowns around a glassy sea. The words were lovely, golden, glassy sea. But eternity menaced the thin child with boredom.

Odin, the ruler of the gods, lived in Valhalla, Valhöll, the hall of the slaughtered. It was vast. It was roofed with golden shields and had five hundred doors. Its inhabitants were the Einherjar, dead warriors snatched from the battlefield by the hovering shield-maidens, the Valkyrie, at the moment of being killed. Battle was what they had lived for. Battle was their eternal vocation. Every day they went out and fought each other to bitter death. Every evening they were brought back to life and feasted in Valhöll on the roast flesh of the boar Sährimnir, who, when his bones were picked clean and his blood supped up, was resurrected, made solid and snorting again, so that he could again be slaughtered, roast and eaten, day after long day.

The thin child shivered with fear and excitement at the thought of Odin, a god both sinister and dangerous. He was a damaged god, a one-eyed god who had paid with the other eye for the magical knowledge he had drunk from the fountain of Urd, in which the severed head of the Jotun, Mimir, told histories, stories, spells of power, runes of wisdom. Odin was a god who lurked, disguised as an old man in a grey cloak, with a hat pulled over his empty socket. He was a god who asked riddling questions and destroyed those who gave wrong answers. He carried a war-spear, Gungnir, carved with runes which unlocked the secrets of men, beasts and the earth. The spear was fashioned from a branch torn from Yggdrasil itself. It was lopped into shape. It left a wound and a scar.*

Odin was pictured in the Asgard book in the palace of King Geirod who had roped the wrists of the unknown visitor and set him to scorch between two fires. It was a good picture; the black, enigmatic figure squats between the flaming brands, neither smiling nor scowling, but brooding. After eight nights without food or drink, the visitor was given a horn of beer, and began to sing, louder and louder, a song of Asgard and the warriors in Valhöll, of Yggdrasil with its roots in the roots of the world. Then he revealed himself, and the king fell on his own sword. Odin was an unpredictable god who accepted sacrificed men in the form of 'blood-eagles', tied to tree-trunks, their lungs torn back through their ribs. He was a god who had himself endured torture, which had made him stronger, wiser, and more dangerous.

> I know that I hung on a windy tree
> Nine long nights
> Wounded with a spear dedicated to Odin

---

* This part of the story was first told by Richard Wagner.

Myself to myself, on that tree of which
    no man knows
From where its roots run.

No bread did they give me nor drink
    from a horn,
Downwards I peered;
I took up the runes, screaming I took
    them
Then I fell back from there.

Nine mighty spells I learned . . .

Odin was the god of the Wild Hunt. Or of the Raging Host. They rode out through the skies, horses and hounds, hunters and spectral armed men. They never tired and never halted; the horns howled on the wind, the hooves beat, they swirled in dangerous wheeling flocks like monstrous starlings. Odin's horse, Sleipnir, had eight legs: his gallop was thundering. At night, in her blacked-out bedroom, the thin child heard sounds in the sky, a distant whine, a churning of propellers, thunder hanging overhead and then going past. She had seen and heard the crash and conflagration when the airfield near her grandparents' home was bombed. She had cowered in an understairs cupboard as men were taught to cower, flat on the ground, when the Hunt passed by. Odin was the god of death and battle. Not much traffic came through the edges of the small town in which the thin child lived. Most of what there was was referred to as 'Convoys', a word that the thin child thought was synonymous with processions of khaki vehicles, juddering and grinding. Some had young men sitting in the back of trucks, smiling out at the waving children, shaking with the rattling motions. They came and they went. No one was told where. They were 'our boys'. The child thought of her father, burning in the air above North Africa. She did not know where North Africa was. She imagined him with his flaming hair in a flaming black plane, in the racket of propellers. Airmen were the Wild Hunt. They were dangerous. If any hunter dismounted, he crumbled to dust, the child read. It was a good story, a story with meaning, fear and danger were in it, and things out of control.

In the daytime, the bright fields. In the night, doom droning in the sky.

Homo Homini Lupus Est

Then there was Loki. Loki was a being who was neither this nor that. Neither an Ase nor a Jotun, he lived neither in Asgard nor in Jotunheim. The Ases were single-minded beings. They concentrated on battles and food, or in the case of goddesses on beauty, jealousy, rings and necklaces. Iduna the fair lived in the green branches of Yggdrasil and grew the bright apples of youth, which she fed to the gods. Once, when a giant grabbed her and her apples, Loki took the shape of a falcon and carried them home in his talons. Alone among the gods, Loki was a shapeshifter. He ran across the meadows of Midgard in the shape of a lovely mare. This beast distracted the magic horse of the giant who built the walls of Asgard – so well, that she later gave birth to Sleipnir, Odin's eight-legged steed. Loki was a pestering fly, who stole Freya's golden necklace, Brisingamen. He was intimate with secret places.

He disguised himself as an innocent farmgirl, milking cows; he shifted sex as he shifted shape. He was slippery. He wrestled Heimdall the herald in the form of a seal. He was a salmon, leaping up a waterfall, or sliding smoothly under the surface.

The Germans believed his name was related to Lohe, Loge, Logi, flame and fire. He was also known as Loptr, the god of the air. Later Christian writers amalgamated him with Lucifer, Lukifer, the light-bearer, the fallen Son of the Morning, the adversary. He was beautiful, that was always affirmed, but his beauty was hard to fix or to see, for he was always glimmering, flickering, melting, mixing, he was the shape of a shapeless flame, he was the eddying thread of needle-shapes in the shapeless mass of the waterfall. He was the invisible wind that hurried the clouds in billows and ribbons. You could see a bare tree on the skyline bent by the wind, holding up twisted branches and bent twigs, and suddenly its formless form would resolve itself into that of the trickster.

He was amused and dangerous, neither good nor evil. Thor was the classroom bully raised to the scale of growling thunder and whipping rain.

Odin was Power, was in power. Ungraspable Loki flamed amazement and pleased himself.

The gods needed him because he was clever, because he solved problems. When they needed to break bargains they had rashly made, mostly with giants, Loki showed them the way out. He was the god of endings. He provided resolutions for stories – if he chose to. The endings he made often led to more problems.

There are no altars to Loki, no standing stones, he had no cult. In myths he was the third of the trio, Odin, Hodur, Loki. In myths, the most important comes first of three. But in fairy tales, and folklore, where these three gods also play their parts, the rule of three is different; the important player is the third, the *youngest* son, Loki.

He had a wife, in Asgard, Sigyn, who loved him, and two sons, Wali and Narwi.

But he was an outsider, with a need for the inordinate.

The thin child, reading and rereading the tales, neither loved nor hated the people in them – they were not 'characters' into whose doings she could insert her own imagination. As a reader, she was a solemn, occasionally troubled, occasionally gleeful onlooker. But she almost made an exception for Loki. Alone among all these beings he had humour and wit. His changeable shapes were attractive, his cleverness had charm. He made her uneasy, but she had feelings about him, whereas the others, Odin, Thor, Baldur the beautiful, were as they were, their shapes set, wise, strong, lovely.

> Eastward the old one   in the Iron Wood
> raises the wolves   of Fenrir's race
> one is destined   to be some day
> the monstrous beast   who destroys the moon.

The Iron Wood was outside the walls of Asgard, outside the meadow of Midgard, a dark place, a devilish place, inhabited by things that were part-beast and part-human, or even part-god, or part-demon. The old one in the poem is Angurboda, Angrboða, bringer of anguish, a giant with a fierce face, a pelt of wolf-hair, clawed hands and feet, and sharp teeth. Loki played with her, rippling like flame over and in her body, pleasuring her against her will, clutching and clasping and escaping, invading and ungraspable. They spoke to each other in snarls and hissings. Sigyn would not have known this ferocious Loki or recognised his triumphant howl as his seed went in. Did he foresee the shapes of his children? One was a wolf-cub, armed already with an array of sharp teeth and a dark throat behind them. One was a supple snake, with a crown of fleshy feelers and teeth sharp as her brother's, though fine as needles. She was dull gold with blood-red flickering over her scales as she stretched and coiled.

The third was a woman, or a giantess, or a goddess. She was a strange colour, or colours. Her form was uncompromising, straight-spined, with long legs, strong, capable hands, firm feet. Her face was, there was no other way of putting it, severe. She had carved cheeks and a wide, unsmiling mouth, inside which were strong sharp teeth, wolfish teeth, teeth for ripping. Her nose was fine and her brows were dusky, like smoke, like the lower world's kenning for 'forest', seaweed of the hills. Her eye-sockets went back and back. Inside their caverns were unblinking dark, dark eyes, like pools of tar, or wells where no light was reflected. But the colour. Half of her was black, and half of her was blue. Half of her, those who saw her also reported, was living flesh, and half was dead.

Sometimes the line between the black and the blue split her cleanly, running from the crown of her black head, down the long nose, the chin, the breastbone, the sex, to the space between the feet. But sometimes the black and the blue floated on and in each other. They were beautiful, like the last blue of the sky meeting the dark of the coming night. They were hideous, the colour of bruises on battered or moribund flesh. She slept naked, coiled and curled with her terrible kin, scales, fur, snout, fangs, lids over glaring eyes. They emitted a raucous hissing and purring. They delighted Loki. He fed them and watched them grow. Who knew what they might do? They grew, and grew.

Odin sat on his throne, Hlidskialf, holding his spear, Gungnir, surveying Asgard, Midgard, Jotunheim and Ironwood. Two black ravens, Hugin (thought) and Munin (memory), told him what they had seen during their flight. He turned his fierce face towards Ironwood.

Loki was, in the beginning, in the days when the Gap was flooded by Ymir's pouring blood, the foster brother of Odin. They had sworn blood-brotherhood, and ridden in the same boat over the blood. Now Odin imposed order, and Loki smiled at disorder. The gods knew that the three monsters were dangerous and would be more dangerous. Odin sent out a force to fetch them, Hermodur the bright, and the god of the hunt, Tyr. They crossed the bright bridge, Bifröst, which joins Asgard to other worlds, crossed the river Ifing and came to where Loki was, in the dark land of the Hrimthurses. They seized the three and carried them back to the steps of Hlidskialf. The wolf yawned. The snake coiled herself into a knot. Hel stood rigid, blue-black, staring.

Odin acted. He threw two of the three out into space. The small snake gleamed dully in the air, and fell, and flew, and fell, and came down on the surface of the bright-black ocean that surrounded Midgard. She stretched, and swam for a time, rising and falling on the waves. Then she sank, or plunged, and was out of sight. The gods applauded.

Odin took Hel and flung her towards Niflheim, the dark land of mists and cold. She remained rigid, like an arrow from a bow, a sharp-nosed missile, on and on, down and down, nine days falling through sunlight, moonlight and starlight, past the racing chariots of the Sun and the Moon, past the tips of firs and past their roots, into and through the lightless bogs and swamps of Nifl-heim, across the cold torrent of Giöll and into Helheim, where she was to rule over those human dead who were not fortunate enough to die in battle, a land of shadows. The bridge over Giöll was gold, and the perimeter fence of Hel was iron, high and impassable. Inside the dark hall a throne waited for the bruised, livid being, the goddess, the monstrous child, and a crown lay on a black cushion, made of white gold, and moonstones, pearls like congealed tears and crystals, like frost. When she took up the crown, and the wand which lay beside it, the dead began to flood into her hall like whispering bats, innumerable, insubstantial. She welcomed them, unsmiling. They wheeled about her, whistling weakly, and she had dishes brought, with the ghosts of fruits and flesh, and beakers, inside which were the ghosts of mead and wine, with ghostly bubbles at the rim.

And the wolf? Wolves run strongly through the forests of the mind. Humans heard the howling in the dark, an urgent music, a gleeful reciprocal chorus; the loping, padding, tireless runners are both out of sight and inside the head. There, too, are the bristling coat, the snout, the teeth, the blood. Firelight, and the light of the full moon, are reflected in inhuman eyes, glittering in the dark, specks of brightness in deep shadows. Humans respect wolves, the closeness and warmth of the pack, the ingenuity of the chase, the calling and growling, messages from the throat. Odin in Asgard had two tamed cubs at his feet, to which he threw the meat he did not eat. Wolves are free and monstrous: wolves are the forebears of dogs, which are creatures of the hearth and hunt, who have replaced the pack leader with a human one. Humans and gods made their own packs to hunt down and kill the wolf packs. Maybe cubs were taken from a lair when the parents had been slaughtered, and fed on milk and meat, and brought in from the wild. Maybe a solitary cub sat on its haunches at the edge of a clearing and howled, and was taken in by a woman, and fed and tamed. They point their snouts at the moon, and howl.

The god, Tyr, was a hunter and a fighter. He wore a wolfskin as a cloak; the great dead head lolled above his bearded face, hairy, blind and snarling. When Odin hesitated over how to dispose

of the Fenris-cub, Tyr said he would take it, and
feed it, and tame it perhaps, so it could hunt with
him. Fenris growled in his throat and laid back
his ears. The thin child in wartime wondered why
omniscient Odin did not simply destroy the wolf
and the snake, who were clearly venomous and
appalling, and full of animosity towards the Ases.
But he clearly could not do this – he was
constrained by some other power, which gave
shape to the story that held him. The story
decided that the destroyers must survive. All the
gods could do was inhibit the monsters, disable
them. Tyr believed he knew the wolf, because he
knew the wild. He took him to the woods of
Midgard, fed him, and ran with him through the
trees. They played together: when the beast was
bigger, they would hunt together.

The wolf grew. Like his father he was inordinate. His voice deepened and opened out – he had
a gamut of growls, chuckling barks, full-throated
howls which could be heard, louder and louder, in
faraway Asgard. Tyr heard it as the music of the
wild. He was the only one. The playful cub became
a lolloping youngling the size of a boar, and
growing every day. He killed for pleasure, which

Tyr put down to juvenile playfulness. He left bleeding hares in the snow, and gutted fawns in the forest. He grew to the size of an ass, a colt, and then a young bull. Midgard resounded to his racket, and his silences were ominous, because when he was silent, he was stalking, and no one – no god – knew what he would take it into his head to stalk next. Tyr brought him flanks of pork, and dead geese, to placate him, to have his confidence. Fenris swallowed, and howled, and killed.

The gods decided to tie up the wolf. The words men used to describe the gods were the words they used for fetters or bonds, things which held the world together, within bounds, preventing the breakout of chaos and disorder. Odin ruled with a spear, wrought from a branch torn from Yggdrasil, a spear carved with the runes of justice, a spear which had brought war into the world, to solve disputes, a spear which finished off warriors and was their way into Valhalla and eternal roast pork, honey and chess-play. The gods controlled. The wolf was the raging son of the incomprehensible and unpredictable Loki, who mocked their solemnities and said they would come to no good end.

But something in their sense of the order of things led them to decide merely to restrict and torture the great beast, not to try to slay him. To do this they needed guile, they needed to trick him into co-operating, they needed him to submit.

They made a strong fetter, which was named Leyding, and they went in a gang to the wolf in the woods, and spoke to him pleasantly and said they had brought this plaything for him, to show off his power. They would bind him in it, for fun, and he would break out, and show them the power of his sinews and nerves. The wolf's hackles rose: he looked at them with cold, calculating eyes, the pupils narrowed to pinshots. He could do that, he said, rolling his wiry muscles under his glistening hair. But why should he? They had been betting, they said, facing the beast at the edge of the clearing, from where he could vanish into the dark wood, or spring tooth and claw upon the gods – they had been betting on how long the breakout would take him. Heimdall, the herald, who guarded the high gate of Asgard, could hear the grass grow on the earth, and the wool springing from the hide of sheep. He could hear the wolf's blood pounding and pumping, he could hear his pelt expanding.

'Play with us', he said to the beast, who took a calculating look at Leyding and lay down on the forest floor and held out his great clawed pads. So they took the fetter, and bound his feet, trussed them together, bound his jaw, avoiding the smell of his hot meaty breath, and left him like an ox made ready for roasting. He made a strangled sound, and shook his head from side to side, and coughed in his constricted throat, and coughed again, and shook himself, swelling all his joints, and the fetter cracked and buckled and fell to the earth. The wolf stood on his feet and glowered at the gods and made a sound between howl and purr, which they knew was laughter. He looked at them, almost expecting further play, but they fell back and returned to Asgard.

They told their smiths they must do better. They made a new chain, with double links, cleverly fused together. Its name was Dromi. They took this to the wolf, who put his head on one side, measuring its strength. He said it was very strong. He said also that he himself had increased in size since he shattered Leyding. He would be a famous beast, said the gods, if he could deal with such an intricate piece of smithcraft. He stood and

– 54 –

thought, and told them that this chain was indeed stronger. But then, he himself was also stronger. So he allowed them to truss him again. And then he shook himself violently, twisted and strained, kicked with his feet and broke the fetter into fragments which flew this way and that. And he smiled at the gods, his tongue lolling out, and snickered. And went on growing; Heimdall could hear him.

The gods sent Skirnir, a young messenger, down to the dwarves, who lived deep down in the home of the dark-elves. And the dwarves made a supple skein from unthings. There were six, woven together: the sound of a cat's footfall, the beard of a woman, the roots of a mountain, the sinews of a bear, the breath of a fish and the spittle of a bird. The thing was light as air and smooth as silk, a long, delicate ribbon. This they took to the wolf, to whom they said with cunning that this band was tougher than it looked. They tore at it with their own hands, one after the other, and it was unmarked. The wolf was suspicious. He wanted to decline, and feared they would mock him. He told them that he suspected them of bad faith. Of trickery. He would play this game if one of them placed his hand in between his jaws, as a gage of honesty, of their bond of good faith. Then Tyr put his hand on the hot head of the beast, as he would with a nervous hound, and then put his hand quietly into Fenris's mouth. And the gods wound their floating ribbon round and round flanks and thighs, pads and claws, neck and rump. And the beast shook himself, and twisted himself, and the fetter clung and tightened. This was inevitable. And it was inevitable that he should snap his teeth together, slicing through flesh, skin and bone. And the gods watched the wolf gnash and swallow, and they bound Tyr's bleeding stump. The wolf glared, and said that if a god's hand can be eaten, it will be possible, in the time of the wolf, to kill the gods. The gods' answer to this was to take the cord which was part of Gleipnir – the name of this rope was Gelgia – and thread it through a great stone slab, which also has a name, Giöll. And this they drove into the earth, and attached to another great rock, Thviti. The wolf howled horribly, and gnashed his teeth. So the laughing gods took a great sword and thrust it into his mouth. The hilt is lodged against his lower gums; the point in the upper ones. The great beast writhes in pain, and amongst his howling a river springs from his open jaws. Its name is Hope.

Hope for what?

The gods knew, Odin knew, that the time of the wolf would come. The wolf would join his kin at the end of things. Terrors were foreseen, like the loosing of the wolf, or hound, Garm, which was the watchdog at the gate of Hel's underground kingdom. This beast was related to the two wolves who raced perpetually through the firmament in the skull of Ymir, following the chariots of the sun and moon. The thin child, reading about the solid world that was made when Ymir was dismembered, had seen an engraving of day and night, sun and moon, in racing chariots with fine horses. They went so relentlessly fast, the thin child saw and understood, because they lived in perpetual fear. Behind the sun, behind the moon, were wolves stretched out in full gallop, their hackles bristling, their tongues lolling, untiring, as wolves are in pursuit, waiting for their prey to falter or stumble. Where these terrible creatures had come from, the thin child did not know. The legends said they were the progeny of the dour giantess in Ironwood, kin of the Fenris-Wolf. In the thin child's mind, there must have been a time when the sun and the moon, created by the gods, moved at their own sweet will, meandering maybe, pausing maybe, extending a lovely day, or a lovely summer, maybe, or a dark dreamless night. In one ancient tale the wolves had names. Skoll pursued the sun, and Hati Hrodvitnisson galloped on, intent on catching the moon. The movement of light and dark, the order of day and night and the seasons, was thus, the thin child understood, a product of fright, of the wolves in the mind. Order came from bonds and threatening teeth and claws. The thin child in wartime read, grimly, the prophecy of yet another mighty wolf to come, Moongarm, who would fill himself with the lifeblood of everyone that dies, would swallow the heavenly bodies and spatter the heaven and all the skies with blood. And this would disturb and derange the heat and light of the sun, and give rise to violent winds, which would rage everywhere and destroy forests, and human habitations, and fields and plains. Coasts would be lashed and crumbling, and the stable order of things would shiver.

Jörmungandr

1. The Shallows

The flung snake fell through the firmament in shifting shapes. With her spine locked she was a javelin, swift and smooth, her mane of flesh-fronds streaming back from her sharp skull, her fangs glinting. But she also fell in loops and coils, like a curling whip, like a light ribbon on the eddies of the air. She was angry to have been ripped from her kin. She was a sensuous beast: the rush of air pleased her: she snuffed up the scent of pine forests, heathland, hot desert, the salt of the sea. She saw its restless wrinkles, cream-crested, steel-blue, and met its skin like a diver, head first and the strong tail following smoothly. Down she went, through this new element, down to the sandy floor, stirring up eddies of grains, sliding smoothly between rocky outcrops. She was a land-beast, reared in the Iron Wood; she had played in dark green shadow, coiling in dust. She began to learn saltwater, feeling a new lightness in her muscles, floating lazily to the surface, like silver, like an elver, where the light caught her wet skin. At first she stayed in the shallows, breathing shore air through her blood-red nostrils, making her way through rock pools, sliding along the tidelines, snapping up crabs, limpets and oysters, cracking open razor-fish with her sharp fangs, flicking out the succulent flesh with her forked tongue. She took pleasure in detecting disguise. She noticed the scuttle of hermit crabs, crouching in abandoned shells.

Her sharp eyes, lidless in her sharp head, admired and detected dabs, sprinkled with sand-spots like the sand itself, two black eyes on a flat head like anxious pebbles. She admired the fine edge of the frill of the fin and tail, a shadow-line between sand-skin and sand itself. She blew at the sand, and hooked up the creatures with her spiked tongue. She loved, and sucked, and swallowed, and spat out the debris. She was always hungry, and always killed more than she needed, out of curiosity, out of love, out of insatiable busyness.

She grew therefore. And she grew gills, among her fleshy mane, until she no longer needed to surface for air, or visit the shore unless it amused her.

She had no particular disguise of her own, but in those early days she was hard to see, because her movements were swift and cunning. She was encased in smooth, glassy scales, under which her skin was black, and ruddy, and weed-green as the light caught it, deflected by the scaly armour. She took pleasure in lying in wait in the carpets and cushions of bladderwrack, moving with their sluggish movement as they moved with the tide, going in, sucking out, her coils randomly heaped, as natural as the wet weed, her crown of feelers like a vegetable tuft through which watchful eyes peered.

She played a game of her own in lonely bays. She swam out to the smooth bulk of water, lay along the wave and rode in with it, muscles slack, floating like flotsam or jetsam. When the wave rose in a crest, the snake rose with it, liquid eyes glittering like the coins of sunlight on the surface, arching herself to swoop down with the white water full of air and light until snake and wave hissed on the sand together and rolled idle. After one such plunge she looked upward and saw a cloaked figure, towering above her, a hat pulled over the eyes. For a moment she thought this was one-eyed Odin, come to torment her, and she reared her head back to strike. Then he turned, and peered at her from under his brim, and she saw that it was Loki the dissembler, Loki the quick-witted, Loki her father whose form was hard to remember, even for her, since it changed subtly not only from day to day but from moment to moment. He raised his hat, and his bright curls sprang out. He grinned.

'Well met, daughter. I see you grow, you prosper.'

She coiled herself round his naked ankles. She asked why he was there. He said he had come to see how she did. And to study the wild waves. Whether there was a form in their formlessness. They came in, one after another, in a regular swell. But the water in them was wild, the eddies streamed every which way. Was there an order in the foam? The snake said that it played like needles on her skin, and that that was a delight. The demigod squatted down beside her and made a line of wet pebbles and translucent rainbow shells. He said he had a project to map the shore-line. Not in great regular half-moons as gods and men might draw this bay, to make a haven for dragon-ships. But small, stone by stone, rivulet by rivulet, promontory by promontory, even as small as these fingers, even as fine as a fingernail. A map for sand-fleas and sand-eels, for everything hangs together, and the world may be destroyed by too much attention, or too little care, towards a sand-eel, for example. 'Therefore', said Loki the mocker, to the snake his daughter, 'we need to know everything, or at least as much as we can. The gods have secret runes to help in the hunt, or give victory in battle. They hammer, they slash. They do not study. I study. I know.' He kicked aside his brief barrier, into the plate-lets of water. He listened with his fingertips, scraped away sand, tugged out a bristling lugworm, black and jerking, which he offered to his daughter, who sucked it in.

2. The Depths

After this meeting she met him often, not only where the dry land met the water, but also in the depths. In her hungry journeys she brushed against human hooks, snaking down on long lines, and against cages and netted pouches out of which living things stared, furious, resigned, stupefied. She took pleasure in lifting a fat cod from a bent hook, or in ripping open a basket full of moiling bodies. Some cod she swallowed; some she watched shake themselves and swim away. She let a hundred herring rush from a net and snatched at the next hundred, biting and gulping, leaving blood and bones staining the seawater. Where a hook was impossibly intricate and manifold she rose to the surface to greet the fisher in his spray-streaked cloak. His nets were tied in complicated knots unlike any others; she would swim in huge circles round his boat, waiting for his call, and then rise, streaming wet, and laughing as snakes laugh.

They played a game of disguise and recognition. 'Catch me', he said, and vanished, leaving the dissolving shadow of his cloak against the blue sky. He was hard to find when he was a mackerel, a single insignificant mackerel, away from the shoal. A mackerel's skin is a vanishing trick. Along its sleekness are lines of water ripples, imitating sun and shadow, cloud light and moonlight dropping through the thick water, imitating trailing weed and rushing waves flickering as the mirror-scales twist. He was there, this visibly invisible fish, and when she made a dash he was a patch of daylight, or nightlight, staining the water only, not solid. He led her to the shoals of mackerel, shimmering and speeding, and changed himself to a spearfish, a swordfish, to join the snake in the pursuit. The rushing shoal was like an immense single creature, huge-bellied, boiling, twisting and turning, green and pink and indigo and steely. The snake and the shapeshifter herded the wild fish for the sheer pleasure of the changing shapes of the turmoil. Then they plunged in, again and again, dividing the entity into spinning segments, catching at stragglers, supping them up, rushing the wheeling flank and swallowing the whole of it. The snake was always hungry because she was always growing. She had been like the muscle of a man's arm, and then like a hard thigh, and still she swelled, one long hawser of pure muscle smacking the surface when she rose and fell, bruising the weeds as she pushed her way through, grinding the things that grew on the sea floor.

Her gaping jaw opened wider; her terrible teeth grew stronger and sharper, thickened by the swal-

lowed skeletons and shells of myriads of underwater creatures.

She surged round the world, from icy pole to icy
pole, or through the hot oceans under the burning
sun. She swam under ice-shelves, in aquamarine
tunnels and spyholes, fastening her fangs on the
wings of a diving albatross, spitting out the matted
fur of a plump seal pup. She swam in mangrove
swamps, amongst the maze of roots in the mud,
snapping up fiddler-crabs and mudskippers, spitting shell into the inspissated mess of mud, leaf
skeletons, seaweed. She lay in the mud, staring
up, and watched the shapes of humans, pouring
poison over the surface so that the fish gasped,
stiffened and floated upwards. She made lazy movements and swallowed, fat fish and poison together.

She swam on, meeting miles of floating jelly-
fish, pulsing glassy umbrellas, trailing fine
poisonous filaments, all of which she sucked in,
indiscriminate. The poison did her no harm. But
it collected in sacs behind her fangs; it ran like
quicksilver in her blood. She spat her venom into
the eyes of porpoises and monk seals, blinding
them, swallowing them, spitting out undigested

stuff which sank slowly and swayed in the currents. Once, she dived and pursued a stingray, a vast, flat, smoky beast with a whiplash tail and half-hidden eyes. But something in its motion made her hold off, with her head poised to strike, and the ray, briefly, failed to hold its elegant shape. It dissolved into inky shadows, like veils, and re-formed as a small shark, oil-grey, grinning, and she saw it was her father.

Once, by accident, worming her way through the kelp forest, she came upon Rándrasill and its underwater gardens. It is possible that the sea-tree was not always in the same place: the great snake had traversed the weed-beds many times and had not seen the golden fronds, the amber stipe, the gigantic holdfast. This first time, she was the size of an anaconda in the swamps, the fattest, longest anaconda there could be. Not far from Rándrasill storms whipped up the surface. Not far from Rándrasill underwater craters spouted crimson and scarlet pumice and thick black smoke. But here, everything was as it was, everything was abundant. Sponges, anemones, worms, crayfish, snails of every colour, ruby, chalky, jet, butter-yellow, sea slugs magnificently striped and mottled, supping up jelly from the fronds. Abalone were anchored round the holdfast, throngs of the shells in pink, red, green and the most succulent white. Sea urchins, bristling with fine live spines, grazed the thick algae and hundreds of eyes peered out between the sheltering fronds of the great plant as it swayed in the slow currents. Elvers moved like needles through cushions of sargasso. Jörmungandr, lying limp, and staring with delight, picked out the sargasso fish, trailing coloured flags of flesh indistinguishable from the weeds, by its watchful eye, like a pinhead amongst the growths. There were sea-dragons, lurking in the wavering thickets; there were giant kelpfish, with bladed bodies like the thick fronds themselves. Above on the surface things had made nests from the kelp itself. Seabirds floated on cushions; soft-furred otters reclined in weedy hammocks, turning the abalones in their clever hands, sucking out morsels.

Jörmungandr, this first time, watched almost wistfully. She could not enter into this magic thicket: she was already too fat, too heavy. She was like an onlooker, through a street window, staring in from the dark and damp at brilliantly lit treasure trove. She backed off. She bowed her monstrous head and turned away. When she next saw the tree she would be changed utterly.

She grew. She was no longer the size of any earth-snake. She was as long as an estuary, as a road across moorland. She needed more food. She sucked in krill, like the great whales, she swallowed schools of fleeing herrings. She went down into the dark. On the ocean floor were the corpse-coloured monstrous squid and the sperm whales that tore at them with heavy jaws. She was not ready to take on whales, though she ate the remaining flesh on a dead one, swallowing with the tangy blubber whole colonies of burrowing hagfish, their heads deep in the dead beast. She was prepared to take on the long, streaming squid, tearing off tentacles, driving her fangs into the pale eyes, sipping and swallowing in a cloud of ink in the dark lightless water.

She ate now because she was ravening. She was the length and width of a great river. She went round an iceflo and found herself in pursuit of a shadowy flickering beast that turned out to be herself, following herself. Her head which had been sleek was growing craggy and lumpen. She pursued a pod of orcas, who were pursuing a school of dolphins, all of them making arched surges in the cold water. One orca, a little apart from the group, was unusually glistening and polished, black and white, like wet marble. Its huge mouth seemed to be laughing, was laughing, and its eye was improbably ironic. Demon and daughter greeted each other, she with shakes of her snaky crown, he with whistles and clackings, and slappings of flukes.

Orca and snake fished together. They took big fish – the fat, slow, lazy cod, some the size of a man. They were prodigal feeders: they ripped out livers and eggs and discarded fins and bones. Perhaps the most amusing to chase were the bluefin tunny, a warm-blooded, sleek-skinned, speeding race, bright-eyed and shield-shaped, purple and pearly. They came across human traps for these beasts, cities of nets, with intricate entries, corridors and inner chambers, leading one way, to the slaughter-house. The two of them ripped these houses apart, with fang and tooth and muscle, enjoying the rush of liberated fish, smiling at some, swallowing others. They headed the shoals and picked off the fish on the flanks. They caught seals as orcas catch seals, the black and white smiling beast spy-hopping, erect in the water, then lobtailing, slapping with its flukes, so that crabeater seals, leopard seals, basking on flat rocks, were washed away in the commotion of water towards the seasnake's wide grin.

They played together and their play ended in crimson water and choking.

All this time she grew. She was as long as a marching army on land. She was as wide as underwater caverns, stretching away and away into the dark. She spent more and more time in the darkest depths, where no sunlight came, where food was sparse and strangely lit with glowing reds and cobalt blues. She came across mountain ranges in the water, and belching chimneys and columns of hot gas. She sipped at the blank white shrimp down there, and picked the fringed worms from their crevices. Nothing saw her coming, for she was too vast for their senses to measure or expect. She was the size of a chain of firepeaks: her face was as large as a forest of kelp, and draped with things that clung to her fronds, skin, bones, shells, lost hooks and threads of snapped lines. She was heavy, very heavy. She crawled across beds of coral, rosy, green and gold, crushing the creatures, leaving in her wake a surface blanched, chalky, ghostly.

Thor Fishing

She came up from the depths one day and saw a head as horrid as her own, a horned head with glassy eyeballs and a bloody stump, a head with a thick brow and staring nostrils. She raised herself, swaying like the spyhopping orca, and gulped. Inside the bull's gullet was a hook, a heavy hook, a hook for dangling cauldrons. She swallowed it before she had time to see it. It yanked, it pulled, the deadhead went up and the snake-head followed after, bursting through the sea surface in a fountain of stinking spray.

There was a boat, a fishing boat, like many she had wrecked, by accident, in play. In the boat was a frost-giant, grey and silver and bluish, with a massive fall of icy hair and a huge sprouting ashen beard. Attached to the line, attached to the hook, attached to the bull's head was a face as fierce as her own, black with fury and effort, eyes glinting red under thick brows, crowned with fiery hair and surrounded by a flaming red beard. Thor, the thunder god, hauling her in on a rod and line. Up she came, and up, more and more of her, towering like the mast of the boat. She fastened her sore mouth on the bait, and pulled. The rod arched and quivered. The god held fast and the boat twisted in the water. The snake shook her fleshy mane and hissed poison. The god glared, and tugged, and glared. The giant said, 'We're done for.' The sky darkened, clouds piled into black banks, the snake twisted and hissed, the god held fast, as lightning split the cloud cover. Nothing had hurt the snake like this. She threshed the sea-surface and snorted. The line bent the rod, but strong runes held it firm.

Then the giant, whose name was Hymir, moved across the boat, which was full of slapping water, took out a great hunting knife, swiped at the line, and severed it. The snake bellowed and sank. The god, bursting with fury, took his short-handled hammer and hurled it at her head. It struck a blow. Her thick dark blood swirled in the seawater. Then the hammer fell on and down into the dark, and the snake went after it. Hymir said dourly that Thor would regret that blow, and the god swung his fist at the stony head and knocked the giant overboard. The god swam and waded to the beach. The snake rubbed against the rocks, trying to tear out the hook and the trailing line. She coughed up the deadhead, bashing her cathedral-mouth on razor-rocks, and the hook came out, trailing black shreds from her gullet.

The snake was angrier after this meeting. She killed more wantonly, she stove in boat planks, she uprooted sea forests for the pleasure of her rage. Sometime later, in the kelp forest, she came across Rándrasill – not where it had been – in its gold and amber light, its holdfast in the depths, its great stipe buoyed up by cushions of air in bladders under the streamers. She had seen it once with delight. Now she moved in for a massacre, sparing neither bladefish nor seahorses, neither soft otters nor nesting gulls, neither crown-of-thorns starfish nor prickly urchins, nor those smaller jellies and fine eels, slugs and periwinkles which clung to the weed. She tore with her great jaw at the fronds of the weed itself, shaking her mane from side to side, stripping away whole households, wound in the stipe itself. Ripped arms hung limp, stirred and whirled in the water. Everywhere was murky, full of thick eddies of dust.

She travelled on, lumping her vast bulk over coral reefs and colonies of mussels, crushing, grinding. One day, in the dimness, she saw a wavering form, lumpen and twitching, which she took to be a great whale, maybe wounded, resting on the seabed. Jörmungandr, still bad-tempered, eased forward and snapped. The pain was excruciating, and travelled all round the earth, and back to the soft brain in her vast skull. She had met her tail. She was wound round the earth like a girdle. She thought of resting on the sea floor in an eternal knot. Where she was was desolate black basalt, thick empty depth. She raised her head and began to drag herself, and then to swim in long folds. If she was to rest, she would rest in populated waters, she would lie on beds of pearls and corals, where schools of fish floated past to be snapped up, where the shadows of ships danced on the surface, where there was living kelp to rest her head, where there was food and more food for her vast appetite.

Baldur

The thin child considered Baldur the beautiful.
He was a god who was doomed to die – in the
book this was what was told about him. The figure
in the painting of Jesus talking to the animals, all
white gentleness and golden radiance, was also a
god who was doomed to die. This god would come
back to judge the quick and the dead. Or so she
was told. *Asgard and the Gods* had explanatory para-
graphs in which its scholarly German author
discussed solar myths and vegetation myths. The
sun went into the dark at the winter solstice. Plant
life shrunk to its roots under the earth, hard as
iron, as they sang in the carol, water like a stone.
The stories celebrated the return of spring, the
sun high in the sky, leaves bursting out, grass new
and bright green.

Baldur went, but he did not come back. The
thin child sorted in her new mind things that went
and came back, and things that went and did not

come back. Her father with his flaming hair was flying under the hot sun in Africa, and she knew in her soul that he would not come back. She knew it partly because of the things tangibly unsaid when the family at Christmas raised small glasses of cider, and drank to him, and the hope that next Christmas he would come back. There were stories that ended, instead of going in circles and cycles, and the story of the beautiful god was one of those, and she found it grimly satisfactory. Though her readings and rereadings at all times of the year gave it a kind of eternal recurrence. The story ended, but she began it again.

These gods, she understood, were apprehensive gods, fearful gods, right from the beginning. Asgard had defensive walls and sentinels on watch. There was an expectation of doom. There was the lovely Idun, who lived in a green bower amongst the strong branches of Yggdrasil, and gave the gods the golden apples of youth and strength. One day, the story went, for no reason, she disappeared from the tree. The branches of Yggdrasil hung sapless and withered where she had balanced and smiled. No birds sang. The well Odrörir in which the water of life, cold and dark, was watched by the Norns, had sunk and was stagnant.

Odin sent his raven, Hugin (which means thought), to find out where Idun was. The great bird circled, and went down into the dark, into the land of the dark-elves, where he spoke to the dwarf-lords – Dain, whose name meant dead, and Thrain, whose name meant stiff. They were sleeping deeply and could not be roused, but muttered of destruction, darkness, threats and endings. The raven returned with riddling words. The skies were sinking to Ginnungagap. Things were falling apart. Torrents of airs tumbling and swaying. Idun was under the roots of the drooping Ash in the lair of an ancient giant, Narfi, the father of black Night. The gods went and found her there, shivering and speechless. They wrapped her in a white wolfskin, which covered her brow, so that she could not see the living branches from which she had fallen, and she was comforted. The gods questioned Urd, the Norn, standing by the brim of the cauldron of wisdom. What had changed? Had time and death ambushed them? Were they themselves changed? Idun, shivering in her pale pelt, ancient Urd in her flimsy black drapes, seemed like the drowsy dwarves, sodden with sleep. They could not answer, but wept, floods of tears, brimming in their eyes, splashing on their hands. The huge teardrops, one after the other, swollen and then bursting, were like mirrors in which the questioning gods saw only their own anxious faces. Everything was at once sluggish and slow, and speeded up, rushing to some ending.

Bright Baldur too was seized by sleep. He was sluggish, as winter-sleepers are, who cannot wake, who slide backwards into somnolence and dreams. He dreamed of the wolf with his bloody mouth, breaking free of the magic rope that bound him, snapping the sword in his gullet between his vast jaws. He dreamed of the Midgard-serpent, lapped around the world, unknotting her coils and rising above the waves, spitting poison. He dreamed of Hel and her dark halls, her living-and-dead face, her pale crown, the beaker she had prepared for him when he should come to sit down at her side. Most dreams, the thin child knew, are wispy and thin, can be torn away by a determined sleeper, can be reduced to a peepshow or puzzle in which the dreamer is a looker-on, not threatened. But there are gripping dreams of real terror, more real than the world the dreamer wakes to, thick, suffocating, full of hurt and hurt to come, in which the dreamer is the victim of ineluctable harm.

She had dreams of that kind in this wartime. They were sometimes foolish. She dreamed again and again that 'the Germans' were secreted under her metal bedstead, sawing steadily through the legs, so they could grasp her and carry her off. She knew they were there, even when she woke and knew it was absurd. Bus stops and cafés had posters of grey helmets crouched under benches and tea-tables, listening in, waiting to pounce. If they came, the world would end, but she did not, waking, imagine them coming.

She dreamed also that they had taken her parents and tied them up in a hollow in the middle of a dark forest, the Ironwood. They lay, her parents, bound and helpless amongst dead bracken and mulch. The shadowy grey-helmeted Germans moved purposefully about, doing things with metal and ropes which she could not understand. She herself was hidden above the rim of the bowl, looking down on the terrified prisoners, not even wanting to know what the Germans were about

to do. What was fearsome, the thin child understood, was to have helpless parents. It was a chink
in the protective wall round her, so she believed,
conventional childhood. She dreamed what she did
not know, that her parents were afraid and uncer-
tain. She was a thinking child, and worked this
out. It hurt her, unlike most knowledge, which
was strength and pleasure.

She asked herself who were the good and wise
Germans who had written *Asgard and the Gods* to
collect 'our German stories and beliefs'. Whose
was the storytelling voice that gripped her imagination, and tactfully suggested explanations?

Frigg

The goddess Frigg set out to make every thing on the earth, in the air, in the ocean, swear not to harm Baldur. In *Asgard and the Gods*, the German editor quoted Snorri Sturluson's Icelandic Edda. Frigg, the thin child read, received solemn promises that Baldur should not be harmed by fire and water, iron and all kinds of metal, stones, earth, trees, diseases, animals, birds, poison, snakes. The thin child tried to imagine this oath-swearing. Frigg was pictured in the ur-book, tall, stately, imperious, crowned, with very long pale hair, flowing in the wind. She wore a tight chain-mail shirt, a seemly skirt and incongruous Grecian thonged sandals. Did she set out in her chariot, or was she on foot? The thin child had a literal, visual imagination, that was how she was.

She saw the goddess in the chariot, rushing through the sky, calling out to the clouds, which were Ymir's brains, to the forked rods of lightning,

the hailstones and snowstorms and floods, begging
them not to hurt her son, and the thin child imagined those entities pausing a moment in their
rushing, flinging and burning to acquiesce, to hold
off. But the thin child also saw the goddess walking.
Mostly she was travelling down steep paths around
high craggy mountains, the landscapes of the early
fearful stone chaos from which the German book
said men had first made gods and frost-giants,
Hrimthurses. The goddess in a shimmer of gold
light spoke fearlessly to all these inordinate forms
and beseeched them not to harm her son. And
again, there was a moment of quiet, and a stillness
of agreement. The goddess rushed down to the
roots of the mountains, the dark underground
caverns where dragons and great worms gnawed
the roots of the World-Ash, and spoke to the
beasts, and not only to the beasts but to the
shining walls of the caverns, to millstone grit and
basalt, to veins of iron and tin and lead and gold
and silver that were intricately threaded in the
stones. She spoke to the boiling pits of red lava
and the flowing steaming pumice. To sapphires,
diamonds, opals, emeralds, rubies. The thin child,
in an ecstasy of imagination, heard all these

inanimate things whisper and grate and rustle, and promise. Everything was part of *one* world, and it would not hurt Baldur the Beautiful.

Sometimes the thin child imagined the beasts in ordered rows, as they were going into the Ark, or in the early days of creation. Sleek, hairy beasts with snarling lips and rending canine teeth. Black panthers, spotted leopards, striped hyenas, padding lions, tigers burning bright with hot eyes, prancing jackals and of course the wolves, the grey wolves, the stalkers, the allies of the imagined enemy. They all promised, and with them the Bandar log – the howling monkeys – the duck-billed platypus with its lethal tooth, the bears on the ice and in the jungle, with friendly faces that belied their malice, all these promised, along with the predators of the hedgerow, weasel, stoat, badger, ferret, shrew. The creatures who promised bore no relation to the bunny rabbits and sweet squirrels who listened to the divine teacher in the clearing in the woodlands. They were ruthless, red in tooth and claw, hunters and hunted, both at once, but they paused to promise and the goddess breathed more calmly and went on her way. Birds promised, eagles, hawks, kites, jays and magpies, along with bats hanging like folded leather in the caverns, with small mouths that drank blood.

The thin child spent a tremulous time imagining the snakes. She had once seen the cast skin of an adder, with its diamond head. They opened their fangs, and hissed and promised, adder and bushmaster, krait and cobra, the biting snakes and the spitting snakes, the rattlesnakes and the great constricting snakes of the jungle, boa constrictor and anaconda. And there were the sea-snakes, coiling and flashing in the oily sea, and the water predators, muggers and alligators, and then the fish, smooth sharks and gleeful killer whales, giant squid and stinging medusas, and the shoals of tunny and cod. The line stretched out to crack of doom; things promised that could hardly be thought of as harmful, oysters and earwigs, anemones in woods and on coral reefs, grass even, all the hundreds of kinds of grasses. All the harmless-looking or enticing plants that were killers, deadly nightshade, sooty purple, laburnum with dangling sharp yellow blossoms, the gaudy death-cap, the horse mushroom, and the fly-agaric.

Between the trees and the animals Snorri listed diseases. How do you swear a disease to harmlessness?

The thin child suffered dreadfully from asthma. Because of this disease she lay in bed and read encyclopaedias and *Asgard and the Gods*. She imagined the asthma which inhabited her as an alien creature, it was true. It was pure white and flimsy, it spread its parasitic body through her desperate lungs, her spinning brain, it was like roots working their way into stonework, it was a relative of the boa constrictor and the strangling fig. She had to learn how to sit, how to lie, how to hold her ribcage to accommodate its grip. She imagined Frigg speaking urgently to it – do not hurt my son – and the brief moment when it let go, to promise. She imagined the fiery faces of measles and smallpox, hot and greedy, nevertheless promising. Measles had taken over the sack of her skin and broiled there. Chickenpox had burst through her, boiling up in pustules. But they promised Frigg. Not to harm her son.

Everything was held together by these agreements. The surface of the earth was like a great embroidered cloth, or rich tapestry, with an intricately interwoven underside of connected threads. She walked through the fields to school, in spring and in summer. There were borders of flowers round the wheatfields, full of scarlet poppies, blue cornflowers, great white moondaisies, buttercups, cowslips, corn buttercups, lamb's succory and thorow-wax. Broad-leaved spurge, red hemp-nettle, shepherd's purse, shepherd's needle, corn-parsley. In the long grass in the meadow were milkmaids, orchids and knotgrass.

Under the earth worms were busy, millipedes ran, springtails flourished, all kinds of beetles dug burrows and laid eggs. Maggots and caterpillars squirmed; some were eaten by fledglings and harvest mice, some changed miraculously into butterflies, white and gold, umber and purple, bright blue, pale blue, mint-green, spangled with stripes and frills and eyes on black velvet. Up out of the corn came skylarks, spiralling and singing. Plovers tumbled overhead, crying, peewit, peewit. She had bird books and flower books, the thin child, and noted them all, tree sparrow, bullfinch, song thrush, lapwing, linnet, wren. They ate and were eaten, it was true, they faded and vanished as the earth turned, but they came back at the solstice, and always would, whereas Baldur was doomed to die, for all the promises. If her father did not come back, he would never come back.

There is no record of Frigg having asked humans not to harm her son. Maybe they were always helpless when faced with the gods. Maybe they did not count or were in some other story. They were not woven into the gloss and glitter, the relief and shadows of the tapestry.

The thin child knew the promise could not hold. Something, somewhere, must have been missed, must have been forgotten. Stories are ineluctable. At this stage of every story, something must go wrong, be awry, whatever the ending to come. It is not given, even to gods, to take complete, foolproof, *perfect* precautions. There will be a loophole, slippage, a dropped stitch, a moment of weariness or inattention. The goddess called *everything*, everything, to promise not to harm her son. Yet the shape of the story means that he must be harmed.

The gods celebrated the cohesion of earth, air, fire, water and all the creatures in and on these elements. They celebrated as they might have been expected to, with fighting and shouting. They had a kind of playground scuffle in which everyone ganged up on one unarmed victim, only in this case the centre of the scuffle was Baldur the beautiful, Baldur the victim, standing there peaceably, mildly proud of his invulnerability. They threw things at him, all kinds of things, everything they could. Sticks, staves, stones, flint axe-heads, knives, daggers, swords, spears, even in the end Thor's thunder-hammer, and they watched with delight as these things wheeled gracefully like harmless boomerangs and returned to the throwers. The more returned, the more they threw, thicker and faster. This was a good game. It was the best game ever invented. The gods laughed and smiled and threw, and threw again.

An old woman came to see Frigg who was in her palace, Fensalir. Frigg does not appear to have wondered who she was or where she came from. She was just an old woman like any other old woman, indeed an archetypal old woman. If you looked hard at her she was almost too perfect, the web of wrinkles over her face and neck, the intricate folds of her long cloak over her dark dress, a kind of icon of old-womanhood. If she looked at you – even if you were the queen of the Ases – you could not hold her cold grey gaze, but you knew you needed to speak to her, she shimmered with your need to speak to her, almost as though only your need held her shape together. She was Loki the shapeshifter of course, putting out waves of glamour. So Frigg asked, as he needed her to do, what they were all doing in the fields of Asgard, crying out and whooping?

The old woman said they were hurling weapons at Baldur, and that nothing could harm him. She remarked humbly that someone of great power must have persuaded everything not to harm Baldur.

And Frigg said, as she must, as the tale required, that it was she, his mother, who had called everything not to harm him, and had been heard by everything.

'Everything?' said the old woman.

'Well, I noticed a young shoot on a tree to the west of Valhall. It is a thing called mistletoe. I was past it before I saw it, and it was barely alive, with no strength, too young to make a promise.'

And yet, the thin child thought, she must have been worried at some level, or how would she have remembered this insignificant plant at all?

And then, the old woman was simply not there

at all. Maybe she never had been. Frigg's huge
effort had tired her. Her eyes were dazzled. She
listened to the wild shrieking of the happy gods.

Loki went for the mistletoe. Mistletoe is a feeble
killer. It attaches itself to the boughs and branches
of trees and sends fine threads like blind hair-
worms into the rising columns of water which the
leaves on the tree suck up and breathe into the
air. The mistletoe has no branches and no true
leaves: it is a tangle of waxy stems, with strange
key-shaped protrusions and whitish gluey berries
with black seeds visible through the translucent
flesh, like frogspawn, the thin child always thought,
seeing the lumpish globes of the mistletoe dense
on bare branches in winter. Little twigs of it were
pinned to lampholders and over doorways at the
turn of the winter, and you kissed one another
under it because it was evergreen and clinging, it
represented constancy and perpetual liveliness.
Next to the holly in which it was sometimes
wound, it seemed ghostly, almost absent. The holly
was shiny and scarlet and prickly and strong. The
mistletoe was soft, floppy, a yellowish colour that
was like dying leaves. The thin child had been told

about it in Nature Study. She had been warned against eating it: it was poisonous, she was told, though she was also told that birds fed on it and scattered it about by cleaning its glue from their beaks on the bark of branches, and leaving the seeds with the glue.

It could spread over a tree like an overcoat and suck the lifewater from the wood, so that the remaining corpse was a dry prop for the grey-gold fronds.

It was mystical to the druids, she was told, but she could not find out what they did with it. It was associated with sacrifice, including human sacrifice.

Loki tore it gently from its foothold in an ash tree. It squirmed a little in his facile fingers. He stroked it. It made its hosts put out thickets of fine, sickly twig-masses, witches' brooms they were called, and Loki stroked and stroked his fleshy bundle, and pulled, and made hard, and spoke sharp words to it, until he had not a clump but a fine grey pole, still a little luminous, like the round pale fruit, still a curious colour like snakeskin or sharkskin rather than bark, but a pole, which he twirled in his clever hands until it balanced like a javelin and had a fine, fine point like a flint arrow.

Loki, now again in his own bright form, stepped soundlessly into the hurling and howling throng of the gods, avoiding the missiles, aimed or returning. He turned the mistletoe spear in his hand, telling it to keep its shape. He found the one he was looking for, standing apart at the edge of the crowd, his hood pulled over his dark face. This was Hödur, Frigg's other son, as swarthy as Baldur was golden. He had slipped second out of the womb, his eyelids sealed, like a blind kitten. They remained sealed. He was dark to Baldur's day, night to his sunlight. They needed each other. Because he had never seen, he had his own ways of moving around Asgard, feeling for pillars, measuring steps, holding his shadowy head sideways and listening to space. If Baldur asked him what it was like not to see, he would answer, how do I know, since I have never seen. Loki, seeing him now, saw that his head was down, slightly slanted, listening to the uproar of which he was not part. What was it like, inside that skull? Caverns of blackness, or grey thick cloud, or enclosed shining lights? Loki always wanted to know everything, and might have asked, but now he was bent on mischief. For its own sake, because he alone knew how to stop the singing.

'Why do you not join in the games?' he asked Hödur. 'It is a wonder to see Baldur, calm and smiling, in a hail of sharp stones and pointed arrows that turn away from him, and fail. You should play your part.'

'I have no weapon,' said Hödur. 'And, as you well know, I cannot see to take aim.'

'I have here a sleek and princely spear,' said smiling Loki. 'And I can put my hand over yours, to guide your aim. And then, you will have played your part.'

So he took the blind god by the hand, and led him to the front of the crowd. He put the lance in his hand, and closed his own quick fingers over those dark ones.

'Baldur is over there,' said Loki, pointing with the spear itself. 'His breast is bare, he is smiling, he is waiting for your stroke.'

And he raised the other's arm to shoulder height, and drew it back, and loosed his own grip, and said 'So, now. Throw now.'

And Hödur let the hood slip from his dark head, and threw it back, and hurled.

The mistletoe spear hit Baldur's breast and ran through him.

Baldur fell. Blood blossomed and he choked.

Hödur cast about in the sudden silence for Loki. A gnat buzzed by his ear. The shapeshifter was off.

The grief of the gods was appalling. They broke down. They could not speak for weeping. Most affected of all was Odin: gods did not fall dead, and when the loveliest and gentlest god could be killed in a game, worse still was on the way. For a long time the assembled gods stood stupidly, unable to touch the body, or to move it. The bright hair ruffled in the light wind. Dark Hödur stood alone, listening to the sobbing. The thin child closed her eyes and tried to imagine the inside of his head and failed.

Frigg was a mother and also a power. She had set her will to making her son invulnerable, and what had been waiting for him had mocked her. Terrible in grief and rage she refused to be mocked, to be defeated, to accept this end. If he had gone down to the underworld there were powers there who could be bargained with, pleaded with. Even cold Hel would be moved by the fury of Frigg's grief, greater, Frigg knew, than that of any other mother for any other son. This could not be done to her, as it should not have been done to him. The story ran one way, but she would twist it, turn it back on itself, shape its end to her will.

'Who amongst the Ases', she asked in a voice hoarse with sobbing, 'will ride down to Hel and plead with its ruler to send back bright Baldur to Asgard?'

And Hermodur, the watchman, stepped lightly forward, and said he would go. Then Odin said he must ride there on eight-legged Sleipnir, swiftest of horses, leader of the Wild Hunt, Odin's own horse. So Sleipnir was led forward and Hermodur sprang lightly into the saddle, and spurred him on, and they leaped out of the gate of Asgard and headed for Ginnungagap.

The gods could not punish Hödur for slaying his brother, as this had been done in the Thing, a sacred space. But they banished him, beyond Asgard, into the dark forests of Midgard, where he lurked, hiding in the daytime, ranging at night, armed with a great sword given to him by the savage wood demons. The thin child wondered if Frigg mourned this other son, or cared to think how he must feel; did she know how he had been tricked into throwing the mistletoe? The story went ineluctably on, casting a bright light on some things, leaving others, like Hödur, in thick shadow.

Baldur's funeral was one of the brightest, most brilliant parts of the story. His body was carried to the beach, richly dressed, and put on board his huge ship, Hringhorni, with its high curved dragon prow, and its long lean body made of pitch-black planks. There on the beach the ship was set on rollers and piled high with precious things, gold from Valhalla, beakers, pitchers, shields, hauberks, halberds, encrusted with precious stones, wrapped in silks and furs. Food was brought, flesh from the golden boar, wine in sealed vessels. Odin came with the ring, Draupnir, the dripper, a magical arm ring from which, every ninth night, eight new rings drop. Odin bent over the chalk-white face of his dead son, and whispered in his ear. No one knows what he said.

When Baldur's wife, Nanna, saw his body lying in the ship, she gave a great sigh and fell down.

They ran to support her, tried to bring her back, and found that she was dead. So she too was dressed in her best clothes and put beside her husband on his pyre, ready for the burning.

The ship was very heavy. Baldur's horse had been loaded onto it, a great horse, with all its gleaming harness. The gods meant to light the piled logs, set fire to the ship, and roll it out to sea. But it was too heavy. No one could move it.

There was a great crowd of grieving creatures waiting to see the flames spurt. Odin and Frigg, the ravens, Hugin and Munin, and all the valkyries who could not rescue this dead god. There were frost-giants and mountain-giants, light-elves, dark-elves, and the Dises, dire wailing spirits who rode the wind. One of the frost-giants said there was a woman in Jotunheim who was able to root up mountains and shift their sites. Odin nodded and a storm-giant took wings for Jotunheim. The strongwoman's name was Hyrokkin. She came, not on the wings of the storm, but riding a monstrous wolf. Her reins were living vipers. Gods and men, driven by the wolf in the mind, and the snakes at the roots of the tree, had hunted both creatures remorselessly, destroying their lairs and holes,

cleaning them out. And as they hunted the grey
wolves in the forests, slaughtering cubs, spearing
their dams, so Fenris's kindred in the Ironwood
grew wilder and more monstrous. As they crushed
the heads of snakes and trampled on their eggs,
so the kindred of Jörmungander, like the Midgard-
snake herself, accumulated nastier poisons and
grew in cunning. Hyrokkin's wolf was foul and
grinning, with the muscles of a bison. The adders
hissed and squirmed and showed their fangs. The
woman dismounted; the wolf whirled and snarled.
Odin had to order four Berserkers from Valhalla
to restrain it, and even they were afraid of the
sharp-toothed snakes, who had to be held down
with forked branches. Amid the howling and
hissing the big woman trod heavily and easily. She
wore a wolfskin, like Tyr the hunter, the dead head
lolling over her fat face. She smiled without mirth,
and put one hand on the poop of the black ship
and shoved, and it began to career towards the
black sea, so fast that flames burst from the rollers.
She laughed, and her laughter enraged Thor, who
had not been able with all his strength to move
the ship. He raised his hammer to smash her head,
and she put up a heavy fist to defend herself, and

the gathered gods begged for peace, for quiet for the burning. Thor raised his hammer, Miölnir, and called down thunder and lightning to set fire to the ship and its burden. Blue flames licked prow and stern, rich garments and waxy gods, the mane of the terrified horse and the brands heaped round the deathbed. The flames turned scarlet and gold, and rose and roared. Slowly the ship, with its terrible cargo, moved out over the water. Its wake was crimson like blood, and the meeting of sky and sea was a black line, black on black, luridly lit by the huge fire. Thor stood there, dumb, with his hammer uplifted, and a dwarf ran suddenly in front of his feet. Thor kicked at him, and drove him into the thick of the flames. His name was Lit. This is all that is known about him, that his name was Lit, and he ran the wrong way, and was kicked into a fire that roasted him alive.

There was a smell spreading, a smell of burning flesh, godflesh, horseflesh, dwarf flesh, of sweet herbs and scented woods, of boiling wine and melting gold, and seawater steam. It was not the end of things. But it was an end, and the beginning of another end.

Hyrokkin rode away, despite Thor's desire to

put an end to her. Elves and dwarves, warriors and valkyries, wept hot tears. Frigg did not weep. Her will was set on undoing this death and retrieving her dead son.

Hel

Nine days and nights Hermodur rode the eight-legged horse through the kingdom of death, along valleys and ashen paths where there was no light, only grey on grey, solids and shadows, and no sound except the steady tread of the horse hooves. He came to the river, Giöll, which surrounds Hel's home, and is spanned by a golden bridge. This was kept by a giant porter, Mödgud. She stopped Hermodur and asked him why he was there. His single horse, she said, made more noise than all the dead who had earlier ridden across. And his colour was wrong. Too much blood.

Hermodur said he was seeking his dead brother, Baldur. Mödgud told him that Baldur had ridden over the bridge not long ago. And whether he alarmed her, or whether she pitied him, she let him cross the bridge and ride on in the dark towards Hel.

★　★　★

The halls were surrounded with an iron fence, hugely high. Hermodur rode along it, and came to no gate, though he did come to a cavern with a gatekeeper, a monstrous dog, or maybe a deformed wolf, whose jaws dripped blood, whose fangs gnashed, who growled perpetually, hackles high. His name was Garm. Hermodur stared at this snarling creature. He was not here to fight. He turned Odin's horse and spoke to it quietly, backing off. Then he set Sleipnir to jump, and Sleipnir rose up and over the iron fence, and landed surefooted on the other side, in Hel's inner city. There was a noise of grinding and boiling, from the cauldron Hvergelmir, where the dragon Nidhøggr feasted on bad men. Hermodur rode on. The dead stood silently along his road and stared at him, with the red blood running in his cheeks, with his living breath moving in his chest and throat. They were all grey, the dead. They had two expressions – one of impotent rage, and one of mild vacancy. There was no light in their dull eyes. They stared.

Hermodur came to Hel's hall. He dismounted, and went in, leading Sleipnir, whom he was not about to lose. It was a rich hall, hung with gold and silver hangings, and in spite of that sparkle it was dull and foggy and grey. The great hall did not exactly hold its shape. Hermodur felt it as a narrow tunnel, closing on him: as a vast cavern, stretching away into the distance.

Hel was there, seated on her throne, with her black dead flesh, and her livid white flesh, sombre and stern. She was crowned with gold and diamonds, which sparked with light, and then disappeared, like quenched flames. Baldur was next to her, seated on a rich throne, with his wife beside him, and a sumptuous dish of glassy fruits, untouched, before him. His bright face was blanched. His golden beaker of mead was untouched.

Hermodur bowed to the queen of Hel, and said that he had come to beg for Baldur's return to Asgard. Gods and men, and all creatures, were helpless with grief, and needed the young god to bring back their liveliness, their power to hope. Most of all, said Hermodur, the goddess Frigg had asked him to beg Hel for Baldur's return, for she could not live without him. To this, Hel replied that mothers throughout time had learned to live without their sons. Every day young men died and came quietly over her golden bridge. Only in Asgard could they die in battle every day, as a game, and live again to feast in the evening. In the hard world, and in the world of shadows, death was not a game.

But this death, said Hermodur, had diminished the light of the world.

So, said Hel. It is diminished, then.

Baldur sat listless and said nothing. Nanna leaned against his shoulder, but he did not embrace her.

'Tell Frigg,' said Hel, Loki's child, hurled out of Asgard, 'tell Frigg that Baldur may return if every being, every creature, in the heavens and on the earth and in the ocean and under the earth, weeps freely for him. Can she save him through grief, who could not protect him through love? If there is one dry eye, anywhere, Baldur stays here. As you see, he is honoured among the dead, and he is the chief guest at my table.'

Hermodur knew that he must take back this message. He knew also the shape of this story. But then, he thought, Frigg's fierce will, and the ferocity of her love, and the power of her voice,

may twist the shape of the story, and free Baldur
to ride back over the bridge, where no man rode
back. So he bowed his head, and Baldur opened
his pale mouth and held out the magic ring,
Draupnir, which Odin had put by his corpse.
'Hermodur should take it back to Odin,' he said
mildly. 'Hel is full of gold and silver. We have no
need of this.'

Then the Ases sent out messengers, young gods
and wise birds, horsemen and runners, with one
message to the whole web of Midgard, living
and lifeless, warm blood, cold blood, sap and
stone, that they should weep Baldur out of Hel's
power. Dark Hödur wept in his forest lair. Cattle
and sheep stood stolid and bellowed and snorted
and wept. Howling monkeys and rambling bears
brushed tears from their eyes; vipers and rattlers
hissed and were still while the tears welled.
Stalactites and stalagmites dripped; geysirs
mingled warm tears in the boiling steam; the
surfaces of boulders and outcrops sweated tearwater, as they do when they come from frost to
warm weather. There was steam in the forests
and the meadows from dripping leaves; the

surfaces of apples, grapes, pomegranates, snow-berries and dewberries were slippery with weeping. The sky itself was full of thick cloud which was made of tears, and wept. Under the salt surface, in the kelp forest, the creatures crowded on Rándrasill wept salt into salt, crown-of-thorns and purple squid, otters and slugs, whelks and winkles, made drops of salt water run into salt water. The lidless eyes of fish and the eyes of whales deep in blubber brimmed water into water and the sea level rose. So also did all quiet pools and rushy fountains, and even stone horse troughs inside which red threadworms wept for the brightness that was gone. Water climbed inside Yggdrasil's channels and dripped from the soggy leaves onto the damp bark and the wet ground. The gods wept in their gold palace, even finally Frigg, who had been stony and tearless in her great grief. Tears lay like a veil on her face, a sheet of water like those that brim in the flooded grass round rivers that have burst their banks. The earth and the sea and the sky were one thing, which wept as one thing.

Except. Not the mistletoe, this time. Not

anyone or anything forgotten through the negligence of the messengers of the gods. Something, or someone, encountered in a dark, dry, rocky hole in a black desert. The diligent messenger went in bravely through the weeping rockface, into lightless tunnels — still wet — and came at last to a black hole, stuffy, not damp, in which something vast huddled and swayed. Who was the messenger? Someone close to Frigg, maybe Gna her handmaid, a horsewoman who rode out over the world at her behest. The thing in the black hole made a sound like dry leaves, like tinder, its garments rustled and swirled. It was dry as a dry bone in a dry place, and its face was a dry bone face, black as its wrappings, with cavernous eyeholes and a lipless mouth full of black teeth. This, Gna thought, was some mountain giantess. She approached — quietly — and said she was come to ask the cave's inhabitant to weep with the rest of the world, with the whole world together, so that Baldur might return to the land of the living and bring his light with him. She said, 'Who are you, mother?'

'Thöck' said the dry voice inside the dark bones.

The voice ground out:

> 'Thöck must weep with dry eyes
> Over Baldur's ending.
> Neither in life nor in death did I have
>   need of him.
> Let Hel hold what she has.'

Gna found herself out on the trail through the mountains. Everything dripped. She rode back dejected, and told Frigg that something called Thöck would not weep.

'Thöck', said Frigg, 'means darkness, the dark. I do not believe your dry giantess was a giantess, any more than the old woman with the mistletoe was an old woman.'

The spring of the world was gone. There was a rainbow but it was watery and incomplete, patches of hectic colour here and there in the thick cloud, which never seemed to lift. The tides, swelled by tears, were irregular and unpredictable. Things on the earth drooped in their wetness which would not quite dry. Yggdrasil had stains of mould and decay. Rándrasill was scraped bare, in places, by rasping tongues licking up tearwater. A kind of sloth was at the heart of things.

The gods decided that Thöck was Loki in disguise. They blamed Loki for what he had done – the use of the mistletoe – and for many things he had not had a hand in, Baldur's bad dreams, the wayward weather, too much wet, too much scorching, dark days, too much wind. He was an enemy and they decided he was *the* enemy. They would take revenge. They were good at revenge.

Loki's House

Loki had a house in a high place, an eyrie on a cliff overlooking a wild waterfall, Franang, which hurled itself into a deep pool, which overflowed into a rushing stream. His house was simple: it had one room, with four great doors opening in every direction. Sometimes, in the form of a falcon, he perched on the rooftree and looked with eagle eyes in all directions for the chase he knew would come. The house was sparsely furnished; there was a great fire in the centre, under the chimney, and tables, on which the trickster spread things he was studying. Odin had acquired knowledge in danger and pain, and at the cost of an eye. Odin's knowledge was the knowledge of the forces that bound things together, and of the runes that read and controlled those forces. Treaties were inscribed on his straight spear, torn from the living Ash. This spear both kept the peace and upheld the rule of the gods, who, we have seen, were themselves often referred to, by men, with words that meant bonds and fetters. Odin controlled magic, a form of knowledge that controlled things and creatures, including the societies of gods and men. Odin dealt death at a distance to those who displeased him. He interrogated the Norns, and the dead, and the powers under the earth, in the interests of the Ases and the Einherjar. His vengeance was fearful, and the sacrifices made to him were fearful. Culprits and enemies had their bleeding lungs torn out through their ribcages, making them into ghastly 'bloodeagles', twisted and dripping. No creature could meet his one eye. All lowered their gaze.

Loki was interested in things because he was interested in them, and in the way they were in the world, and worked in the world. He was neither kind nor gentle, not anyway when he inhabited the world of myth. In the world of folktales he was a fire demon, mostly benign, providing warmth for hearths and ovens. In the world of Asgard he was smiling and reckless, a forest fire devouring what stood in its path.

In his falcon shape he hunted small creatures and brought them back and spread their brains and lungs on his table so that he could study the forms lurking in the intricate shapelessness of their mass of spongy air-cells, the branching veins, the slits for their roots. Brains, too, amused him. He liked the twining convoluted lumps, white inside, grey outside, and the fissures running between the lobes. A sacrificed man was a cross, a simplified tree. A lung, a brain, was complexity run wild, an unholy mess in which a different kind of order might nevertheless be discerned.

He collected other things which also seemed at first glance formless. A wing feather was regular, hooked plumes sprouting orderly from the spine of the quill. But down – duckdown, swansdown with matted or floating wisps – down was intriguing, there were rhythms and repetitions lurking in the puffed threads.

He studied, most of all, fire and water. Fire was his element but he also changed himself into a great salmon and threaded his way swiftly through the crash of the waterfall, across the eddies of the deep pool, over its lip into the rushing river, which parted round a great stone, and joined again, twisting and bubbling.

You could read the future in columns of smoke, or leaping points of flame, red, yellow, blue-green, never still but holding their shape. Why did the smoke rise smooth and fast in a straight column and then quite suddenly divide into fantastic swirling, more and more turbulent? Why did the water flow smoothly towards the rock, so you could see the fine lines of bubbles smooth in it, or let them run over your shining scales, pink and silver? And then, suddenly, the water round the rock would divide every which way, frothing and spinning in curves and curlicues, occasionally gathering and spinning round sudden whirlpools. The water grew wilder like the smoke, and in many ways resembled it. Loki wanted to learn from it – not exactly to master fire or water, but to map them. But beyond the curiosity there was delight. Chaos pleased him. He liked things to get more and more furious, more wild, more ungraspable, he was at home in turbulence. He would provoke turbulence to please himself and tried to understand it in order to make more of it. He was in burning columns of smoke in battlefields. He was in the fury of rivers bursting their banks, or the waterwalls of high tides throwing themselves over flood defences, bringing down ships and houses.

He was reckless and cunning, both. He swam

in his waterways seeking out hiding places for when the gods came, gravel patches against which the great still fish, scaly and glittering, would not stand out, deep channels along which he could slide towards the sea, churning pools where ripples and sucking obscured the view.

He thought like the gods, to forestall them. If he were a god, and he knew that his enemy was fish-shaped and rapid, how would he trap him? He began, with long strips of twisted linen threads, to make a net that would go across the outlet from the pool, and which would entangle the big fish. He got interested in this, and invented several new kinds of knots, and a kind of drawstring for pulling round the struggling fish. *That* would get it, he thought, and noticed that his fire was suddenly smoking fiercely – a strong, regular flow of smoke, going up and up, and then breaking up into whirling. This was a sign that the pursuit had found him, and was on its way, riding the clouds. He dropped the fishing net hastily into the fire – which sputtered blue and bit into it. Then he became a bird and flew to the waterfall where he became a salmon and swam down deep.

★　★　★

The gaggle of gods, with their flying horses, goat-drawn and even cat-drawn chariots, rode the north wind and broke into the house through all four doors. They looked around: the trickster was not there. One observed that he had recently been there, for the hearth, and the ashes in it, were warm. A very clever god, Kvasir, who was known for making poetry, stepped forward and studied the hot ashes. They were made of wooden logs and bracken tufts, which still held the grey ghosts of their shapes, though when they were touched they would fall into shapelessness. Lying over these burned plants was an ashen pattern, a regular pattern, a pattern of squares and diamonds, and threads and knots. Kvasir scrutinised the knots, told the others to touch nothing, and found Loki's store of linen threads. This was the phantom of a clever trap for fish, Kvasir told the gods. A new one could be put together, after scrutinising the forms of the knotting. So he squatted down, nimble-fingered, and made a new net.

The gods slunk out to the waterfall, carrying the fishnet. The fish heard their tread, and sank to the gravel, moving nothing but his gills. The gods stood round the deep pool and cast the net into it. They could see nothing, for the surface bubbled with turbulence. The fish moved his fins to shift the gravel, and half bury himself, and the cast net went over him. He thought about how he would get out of this, and considered making a dash for the pool lip and the open stream. But they would see him, they were sharp-eyed. Maybe, he thought, he could do what salmon did, and surprise them by making a wild leap *up* the falling water, and swim away, upstream. He was, he was sure, cleverer than all the gods put together and that was not saying much, said the trickster to himself in his proud mind, fanning the gravel. Kvasir however had the idea of weighting the net and dragging it across the floor of the pool, held by Thor on one side, and all the other Aesir on the other. So they did this, moving slowly and resolutely, and they felt the net hit and pull against a solid body. So they pulled the cunning strings and drew him up fighting, the sleek and lissom fish with furious eyes. He was limp until they had him at the rim, and then made a great muscular leap, and would have got away if Thor had not put out a vast hand and gripped him by the tail. The fish struggled.

The thunder god held on, revenging himself for countless taunts and teasing tricks. They wrapped him in the copy of his own burned net, and carried him back to Asgard.

The word for gods is also the word for bonds, and Loki, like his son Fenris, was bound. They took him to a cave and set up three flat stones, and bored a hole through each one. They brought his family to see his defeat – not the inordinate family from the Iron Wood, but his faithful wife Sigyn, and her two sons, Wali and Narwi. They said the shapeshifter should see shapes shifted, and they turned the young man, Wali, into a snarling wolf, who immediately set upon his brother and tore him limb from limb. Then the smiling gods killed the wolf – Odin plunged his great spear, Gungnir, into its guts. Laughing, they took the bloody entrails and sinews of wolf and man, and used them to bind Loki, between the three stones – one under his shoulders, the second under his loins, the third under his knee-joints.

Loki stirred in the dripping web, thinking perhaps that he could still become a fly, or an earwig, and creep away. But the gods sang runes to the bonds of flesh, and they became iron and gripped.

The storm goddess, Skadi, blithe and mocking, brought a vast snake, spitting poison, and caged it on the cave-roof over Loki's face, so that the poisonous spittle dripped endlessly onto him.

There he should stay, the gods said, satisfied, until Ragnarök.

His wife crept up with a great dish, in which she caught the poison. It was said that whenever she had to take this dish away, to empty it, the prisoner writhed in his bonds, and this was what humans felt as earthquakes.

The gods laughed at the pair of them.

But they knew Ragnarök was coming, the thin child thought. The Fenris-Wolf was bound, and Jörmungander was made into a bond, clasped round the earth under the sea. Hel was inside her palisade. Wolves and snakes infested the mind, but were kept within limits. As the snake circled the sea, the sky-wolves circled the heavens, always pursuing Day and Night, Sun and Moon, never catching them, never relenting.

In *Asgard and the Gods* Ragnarök came hard

upon the binding of Loki, as though there were no meaningful events to be recorded in the gap between. The book explained that 'Ragnarök means the darkening of the Regin, i.e. of the gods, hence the Twilight of the Gods; some however explain the word Rök to mean Judgement, i.e. of the gods'. The Twilight is particularly pleasing, though etymologically wrong, it appears – it is Ragnarök, judgement or destiny (ragna is the genitive plural of Regin). Ragnarøkkr would indeed mean twilight of the gods, but it is, we are told, a misreading.

The thin child was baffled by the placing of the death, darkening, judgment, or twilight of the gods in the story book she had. Part of the delight and mystery of this book was that everything was told several times, in different orders and in different tones of voice. The book opened with a kind of headed catalogue of the gods, with their deeds and fates. Ragnarök has its place in this list, appearing as early as page 16, summarised poetically. But it is retold in a more naturalistic form at the end of the book, with emotions and judgments, and it is retold again in a verse translation of the Völuspa, or Wöluspa, the Lay of Wala, at the very end of the book, incantatory and chilling. It is told in the present tense, a prophetic vision of the future, seen as though it was Now. The thin child became an onlooker at the death of the world, every time she read these different tellings of the tale. Even Baldur's bad dreams were a foreseeing of the disasters of Ragnarök. It felt different from Christian accounts of the end of things, with the undead god returning to judge the quick and the dead. Here the gods themselves were judged and found wanting. Who judged? What brought Ragnarök about? Loki, waiting to be found, waiting to be trapped, waiting to be bound, was described as knowing that his torment was the beginning of the time of Ragnarök. He would be tortured until Ragnarök came. No one, the thin child thought to herself, had any doubt that Ragnarök was coming, neither the gods, nor the wolves, nor the snakes, nor the shapeshifting trickster. They were transfixed, staring at it, like rabbits with weasels, with no thoughts of averting it. The Christian God condemned sinful men, and raised up the 'good' dead. The gods of Asgard were punished because they and their world were bad. Not clever enough, and bad. The thin child, thinking of playground cruelty and the Blitz, liked to glance at the idea that gods were bad, that things were bad. That the story had always been there, and the actors had always known it.

LOKI IN CHAINS

THE THIN CHILD IN TIME

Imagining the end of things, when you are a child, is perhaps impossible. The thin child, despite the war that was raging, was more afraid of eternal boredom, of doing nothing that mattered, of day after day going nowhere, than she was of death or the end of things. When she thought of death she thought of the little boy across the road who had died of diabetes. No one at school, told of this, knew how to respond. Some giggled. They shifted in their seats. She did not, in fact, imagine this boy as dead; she went no further than understanding that he was not there and would not be. She knew that her father would not return, but she knew this as a fact in her own life, not in his. He would not be there again. She had nightmares about hangings, appalled that any human being could condemn any other human to live through the time of knowing the end was ineluctably coming.

SURTUR WITH HIS FLAMING SWORD

RAGNARÖK

It began slowly. There were flurries of sharp snow over the fields where the oats and barley were ready to be harvested. There was ice on the dewponds at night, when the harvest moon, huge and red, was still in the sky. There was ice on water jugs and an increasing thin, bitter wind that did not let up, so that they became used to keeping their heads hooded and down. There was a wonderful harvest of frosted grapes, to make the Mosel wine, the eiswein, which was put down in casks. Winter vegetables wilted on their stems, frozen before they were plump. The leaves in the woods and forests fell early, and blew about in the eddies of bitter wind. The light, at first, was clear and cold: things glittered, ice in the cart-tracks, icicles growing on sills and bushes, and not shrinking, not melting, thrusting on. Then, as winter set in, the sky darkened. It was full of thick iron-grey clouds full of snow, and the air itself was full of snow and hail and ice-splinters eddying. The surface of the earth hardened, shrinking and dense, frozen too deep for spades to disturb. Root vegetables could not be lifted, could not be disinterred. Ice thickened on lakes, and spread sluggishly into the courses of rivers. Fish went down and down, swimming at first under the ice-shelves, then settling into the mud, cold and limp, barely breathing. Men went out with axes and hacked off buckets of ice to melt in the house for drinking. At first this excited them. It was a test of strength. A test of manhood. Cattle were enclosed and the sheep brought in, those who did not die in the drifts which rose higher and did not diminish. Hens came into houses, and pigs lay by the hearth. Men went out on snowshoes, and skis, and sledges, and took down trees for firewood, and hunted the increasingly furtive and cunning wood creatures, rabbits and hares, small deer and partridges, small fowl with their feet frozen to the twigs in the bushes.

They needed to survive until the spring. Until the days at last grew longer and the sun would melt the snow and the ice, and the wind would die down, and skins could be in the air without being frostbitten.

The shortest day came, and the humans danced, stamping, in the snow, and made bonfires, to greet the turn of the year.

But the year did not exactly turn. The sky became a paler grey, that was all, and the earth and air and water stayed icy.

They began to use things that could not be replaced. The pig's throat was slit and it was butchered and frozen and roasted. Those hens that did not lay were strangled and plucked and boiled and were not replaced because most chicks died. Feeding the sheep – and the horses and donkeys – became hard – very hard – because of the ruined crops and the frozen fields. Courage became endurance, and soup was needed too much to be fed to the dying.

Outside, in the perpetual twilight, wolves howled and padded. They were hungry and angry.

This, they thought, was how it would be when the Fimbulwinter came. The fat sun was dull red, sullen, like embers. She gave little light, and what there was was ruddy or bloody. They longed in their bones and their brains for clear light, for a warm wind, for buds, for green leaves. The winter stretched into another year, and another. The seas froze:

icebergs clashed by the coasts, and floated into the bays. This was, they began to understand, not a likeness of the Fimbulwinter, but the thing itself.

They became raiders. They overran each others' housesteads, howling and roaring, slaughtering the weak and emptying the meagre stores. They drank what mead there was, swallowed the wine as though there was no tomorrow, which they began to believe was true. Hungry creatures, hungry men, will eat anything. The battle-winners feasted among the dead bodies, which were being torn at by creeping, crouching beasts. They gripped each other and fell about the fire, fornicating with whomever was to hand, with whatever was to hand. They bit and kissed and chewed and swallowed and fought and struggled and waited for the world to end, which it did not, not yet. They ate each other, of course, in the end.

The skies thickened and thickened. Things – Dises – leathery winged female things – wailed in the wind and perched on the crags, staring and screaming. Nidhøggr the great worm who gnawed the roots of Yggdrasil came out and sucked the blood from the dead as they lay in the freezing slime. From the Kettlewood, where Loki lay bound

amongst the geysirs — which still spouted hot —
came a louder howl of wolves, wolves in the wood,
wolves padding over the snow, wolves with blood
on their fangs, wolves in the mind.

Wind Time, Wolf Time, before the World breaks
up.

That was the time they were in.

In Asgard the sheen on the gold was dulled, but
the magic boar could still be eaten at night and
reborn for the next feast. Yggdrasil was shaking
all over, leaves were falling, branches were wilting,
but the tree still stood. Odin went down to the
well at its roots and spoke to Mimir's head under
the black ruffled water. No one ever knew what
he learned, but he came back set and cold. They
waited. They did not act, they did not think,
perhaps could not think. Idun lay, curled in her
wolfskin. The apples of youth were withered and
puckered.

Under the ice the earth boiled. South in Muspelheim the age-old fires raged, and shapeless

fire-creatures wandered, flamed and flickered, as they always had. But now hot rocks, a rain of searing ash, and spreading tongues of glassy lava, red-gold and spitting, turning to red-black and sullen, pushed their way through the hard earth. Red domes rose and rose, bubbling and frothing, breathing death gases, falling on forests, making firewood of them. Loki's place of torment was called the Kettlewood because the stones that tortured him stood in a cave amongst boiling geysirs. Now these blew more and more furiously, spouting cinders, and the earth shook itself, like a beast in great pain, and the shapeshifter's bonds broke. He stood there laughing amid smoke, steam and a whirlwind of tossed stones, and set off south, striding through chaos. He went rapidly through the sacred wood where the Fenris-Wolf was bound, and the soil burst open at his tread, and the trees writhed and fell and the magic rope, Gleipnir, made of the trample of cats, the beards of women, the breath of fish and the spittle of birds, shrivelled and fell apart. Fenris yawned and dislodged the sword from his bleeding gullet. He shook himself and his hairs hissed like fires. Father and son loped on, going south to the land of flame.

Crimson cracks opened under their feet in the thick glaze of the ice. They laughed. They howled with laughter.

The guardian of Muspelheim sat on its borders. His name was Surtr, the Black One. He held a hot sword, too bright to look at, and black smoke swirled round him. He rose to his feet — up and up — and shook his sword and called, and the hosts of Muspelheim, with white-hot weapons and slings of flame, were on the march.

Odin saw them, from his high seat, Hlidskialf. They were roaring on towards a field called Vigrid, a hundred leagues in all directions. This was the moment. This was the beginning of the end. These gods were gods who had existed in waiting, waiting to make a last stand. Heimdall the herald rose up and blew the great horn, Giallarhorn. It had been crafted with this last great cry in mind. The gods rose up and armed themselves, swords, shields, spears, hauberks, glimmering gold, and the Einherjar did the same. Odin went down again and spoke to Mimir's head in the black water, now further blackened with falling soot, which was everywhere. The great tree trembled and shook. The surging earth was loose about its roots. Its branches flailed: leaves were ripped off in the gale and added to the hot air stream: the fountain of Urd began to boil.

The gods went over the bridge, Bifröst, the rainbow bridge that linked Asgard and Midgard. They were damaged already, when they set out. Tyr had lost his arm to the wolf, Odin his eye to Mimir, Freyer had given away his magic sword, Thor's wife, Sif, had seen all her magical hair fall away from her bald head. Thor himself, according to some poets, had lost the hammer he had thrown after the Midgard-serpent. Baldur had lost his life. There are two ways, in stories, of winning battles – to be supremely strong, or to be a gallant forlorn hope. The Ases were neither. They were brave and tarnished.

Yggdrasil drooped. Its leaves hung and flapped. Its roots were shrinking. The columns of water inside the bark were troubled and feeble. The squirrel chattered with fear and the stag's head hung. Black birds spun away from the branches into a red sky.

The sea was as black as basalt, covered with churning foam, ice-green, clotted cream, shivering high walls full of needles of air going up and up and crashing down on other walls of water on the crumbling coasts of the world.

The ship was launched in the east. It was a terrible and a beautiful ship, made of a material buoyant and dully translucent, the horny afterlife of dead men's nails, culled as they pushed out, after the blood stopped. It was a ghost ship, bone-coloured, deathly grey, as though all the floating mess in the water, that would neither rot nor disintegrate, had coagulated and clung into this ramping vessel. Its name was Naglfar. Its helmsman was the giant Hrym. As a small child the thin child had imagined it like a schooner with ghostly rigging and flying pennants. Then she came to see it was a dragon-prowed, long-necked, long-bodied raiding ship, like a dead snakeskin made of layers of scales from the toenails, shining dimly. It was manned by frost-giants and fire-giants, both together, and dashed on in a cloud of boiling steam.

As the crust of the earth boiled and spat, the skin of the sea began to dance madly, with geysirs blowing onto the waves, which were full of floating death, shoals of battered glimmering fish, carcases of whales and narwhals, orcas and giant squid and sea-snakes, all boiling up and torn apart by heat and cold and raw force.

Then, behind the stern of Naglfar the surface of the sea rose in a mountain, immense, streaming, with shifting clefts and gullies, pouring with ripped seaweeds and grains of crushed corals. In the midst of the mountain was the horrid head of Jörmungander, the Midgardsomr, the band of snakeflesh that held the solid world in shape. Up and out she came, uncoiling and driving, her fleshy mane towering, her vast tail rising from rock and sand, stirring the whole sea. Naglfar floated lightly on the maelstrom of her motion, and Hrym, the frost-giant, shook his axe to greet the monster. Her body was wound in ripped-up weeds and dead men's ropes and chains, with the dead men still dangling and gaping. She began to writhe in the water, making purposefully for the battlefield, Vigrid. Like her father and brother the great snake laughed out loud, and poison dripped from her fangs and made flames on the crests of the waves. Vast surges of seawater overran the coasts, beaches, rocks, harbour walls, delta, estuary, marsh. The world was unrecognisable.

When the bond round the earth was loosed,

other bonds broke. The hell-hound, Garm, snapped his chain and leaped out to join his wolf kindred. The sun in her chariot, and the moon in his, whipped up their horses in their everlasting rush round the sky. But the tireless pursuing wolves, joined by Garm, with crimson eyes and gullet, knew that their time had come, galloped faster, and fastened their teeth in the haunches of the silver horse and the swarthy. The horses screamed and swerved, and light in the world went mad, black, blazing white, dark as hell, lurid red. The wolves tore the throats out of the horses and turned to the drivers of the chariots, sun-woman, night-mother, moon-boy and the boy in the bright chariot of day. Somewhere in the middle air, as the chariots rolled in their fall, the wolves tore apart sun and moon, day and night, drank their blood and swallowed them.

The stars, it was thought by some, were an outer light, shining through holes in Ymir's dead skull. But now, as the wolves began to lope, laughing, through the sky towards Vigrid, the light began to drop out of the stars, they fell like spent candles or dead fireworks, raining down on the burning and boiling earth. Fenris saw his sky-brothers and howled to greet them. He had grown. His snout scraped Ymir's skull and his jaw lay along the singed earth.

The gods and the warriors of Valhall advanced like berserkers onto the battle plain. They roared defiance – this was what they knew how to do – and the wolves, the snakes, the fire-giants and the frost-giants howled and hissed back, whilst Loki stood smiling in the leaping light of the red flames, which was all the light there was.

Odin advanced on the Fenris-Wolf, balancing his ash-spear, Gungnir. The wolf's hackles bristled. His mean eyes glittered. He yawned. The god drove the spear into the gaping jaws. The wolf shook himself, snapped the spear, took three steps forward, gripped the great god, shook him, broke him, swallowed him. Wailing swept through the Einherjar. They staggered, fell back, and then advanced again, mute now. There was nothing else to do.

Loki's children towered over the field, the wolf-laughter joining the hissing mirth of the snake. Thor, full of grief, threw himself at the snake with flailing fists and a thunderous hammer, breaking her skull. She writhed, fell and spat poison. Thor turned to tell the gods all was not lost, the snake was down. He lived for nine paces in the stream of poison she had poured over him, and then fell, dead.

There were other duels. One-armed Tyr, still in his wolfskin, fought with the hell-hound, Garm, until both were exhausted and beaten down, never to rise again. Freyer was despatched by the bright sword of Surtr. A young son of Odin, whose name was Widar, crept across corpses and stabbed the Fenris-Wolf through his blooded pelt. The wolf coughed and fell, smothering the avenger under his weight.

Loki watched the kills and killing of his monstrous children. Then, as the battlefield began to settle into a welter of bloody slime, he fenced with Heimdall, the herald, the far-sighted, both with the recklessness and eagerness of the doomed. They killed each other; their bodies fell across each other and were still.

The earth was Surtr's. His flames licked the wounded branches of Yggdrasil and shrivelled the deep roots. The homes of the gods fell into the lake of fire. Grieving Frigg, on her gold throne, sat and waited as the flames licked her door sills and ate up the foundations of the house. Unmoving she flared, shrank black, and became ash amongst the falling ash.

Deep in the kelp forests Surtr's fire boiled in the foundations of the sea. The holdfast of Rándrasill ripped loose and its lovely fronds lost colour, lost life, tossed in the seething water amongst the dead creatures it had once sheltered and sustained.

After a long time, the fire too died. All there was was a flat surface of black liquid glinting in the small pale points of light that still came through the starholes. A few gold chessmen floated and bobbed on the dark ripples.

RAGNARÖK, THE LAST BATTLE

THE THIN CHILD IN PEACETIME

The thin child stored this picture of the end of things, like a thin oval sliver of black basalt or slate, which was perpetually polished in her brain, next to the grey ghost of the wolf in the mind, and the gleaming coils and blunt snout of the snake in the mind. She read for what she needed, and chose not to imagine, not to remember, the return of gods and men to the refurbished green plain of Ida, which was related in *Asgard and the Gods*. The careful German editor of that book observed that this resurrection was probably a Christian contamination of the original bald end. That was enough for the thin child. She believed him immediately. What she needed was the original end, the dark water over everything.

The black thing in her brain and the dark water on the page were the same thing, a form of knowledge. This is how myths work. They are things, creatures, stories, inhabiting the mind. They

cannot be explained and do not explain; they are
neither creeds nor allegories. The black was now
in the thin child's head and was part of the way
she took in every new thing she encountered.

She had stored Ragnarök against the time when
it would become clear that her father would not
come back. Instead, one night, after midnight,
when the blackout was still over the windows, he
came back, unexpected and unannounced. The
thin child was woken, and there he was, standing
in the doorway, his red-gold hair shining, gold
wings on his tunic, his arms out to hold her as
she leaped at him. Walls of defence against disaster
crumbled in the thin child's head, but the knowledge of Ragnarök, the black disk, held its place.

They went back home, the thin child and the
family. Home was a large grey house with a precip-
itous garden in the steel city, which had its own
atmosphere which could be perceived as a wall of
opaque sulphurous cloud, as they came in from
the countryside to which they had been evacuated.
The thin child's lungs tightened desperately as
the fug closed in on her.

There was something of Bunyan's allegory about the places to which they returned. The old house was in Meadow Bank Avenue, an oval space like a long pan, from which a steep, narrow path sloped down to a place called Nether Edge. The thin child was quite a bit older when she understood the beauty of the words, Nether Edge, as opposed to just saying them quickly and thinking of the place where the butcher had his shop, with his hatchets and knives and bloody limbs of creatures, where the huge buses raced and boomed, where the stationer sold sherbet, newspapers and gobstoppers.

In the midst of Meadow Bank Avenue was a large oval patch of grass which was the Green, surrounded by a low fat grey stone wall on which you could sit. At one end was a group of tall trees, beech and oak. It must once have been a village green, where Blake's children were heard at play. Modern children still played on it, but it had been immured in the spread of suburb.

The thin child's father, in his spare time, which diminished as he became more and more successful, took to building a garden. There was a small flat lawn and a wash house, behind the house, and at the end of this exiguous lawn a wooden arch which the child remembered from the days of her infancy, an archetypal arch, covered with archetypal roses, red, white, sugar-pink. Under the arch the garden fell precipitately down towards Nether Edge. The roses had run wild in the war. They spread in thorny thickets like those in fairy tales. The thin child's father, singing as he worked, curbed and trained them, fastened them to the rustic poles of the arch, licked his pricked fingers and laughed. He ordered stones from the countryside, grey stones like those which were cleverly built into the walls that kept in the moorland sheep. He began to set the plunging garden in order with dry-stone stepped terraces, holding in flowerbeds with lilies, Shirley poppies, rose bushes, lavender, thyme and rosemary. He made a pool from an old stone sink, in which swam tadpoles and a stickleback the thin child caught in a net on a picnic, a furious red swimmer she named Umslopogaas. It was a pretty garden in its newness, despite the soot in the air. The thin child loved her father, and loved the garden, and wheezed.

The thin child's mother, who had been gallant and resourceful in wartime, might have been expected to find a happy ending in the return to the comfortable home from which she had been exiled. In fact she suffered what the thin child, much later, learned to call a fall into the quotidian. She was not a mother who had ever been any good at playing with her children, and the thin child could not remember her reading aloud, however inexhaustible the books and stories she gave the child. During the war, when she was teaching, she had had friends. There was Marian who wore a green hat with a dashing pheasant feather and played games of Robin Hood, running through woodland, shooting bows and arrows. The thin child's mother looked on, in an agony of embarrassment and uncertainty about this behaviour. The thin child watched her mother, and took notes. But her mother did inhabit the countryside and its stories. The boys she taught clearly loved her. They gave her living creatures – a hedgehog dripping fleas on the carpet, a tank full of great crested newts who tried to escape at breeding time and died, shrivelled, under the gas cooker. The hedgehog was released into the field at the bottom of the garden, and its donor was told it had escaped. He brought another, equally flea-ridden,

the next day, which was also released. There were
vast slimy clumps of frogspawn, and then tanks
full of inky tadpoles who ate each other. The thin
child's mother went on walks, in those days, and
lovingly named all the flowers. The thin child had
a complete collection of books of Flower Fairies
with well-written verses and elegant pictures.
Dogrose, Lords and Ladies, Deadly Nightshade,
violets, snowdrops and primroses.

The long-awaited return took the life out of
the thin child's mother, the thin child decided
many years later. Dailiness defeated her. She made
herself lonely and slept in the afternoons, saying
she was suffering from neuralgia and sick head-
aches. The thin child came to identify the word
'housewife' with the word 'prisoner'. Fear of
imprisonment haunted the thin child, although
she did not quite acknowledge this.

The outdoor spaces of her wartime, the wheat-
field, the meadow, the ash tree, the hawthorn, the
hedgerow, the muddy pond, the tangled bank,
became a thing in her mind like the black slate or
basalt. They were compressed to a spherical tuft
with pushing roots and shoots, with creeping,
crawling, flying and swimming things, with a patch

of fierce blue sky, another of green grass, another of golden corn, and another of the dark earth under the dense hedge. It was a small world, into which she had been exiled or evacuated. It was the earthly paradise that once had been.

She still read in bed at night, returning often still to *Asgard and the Gods*, and to *The Pilgrim's Progress*, lying on her stomach in her bedroom doorway to catch the landing light on the pages, creeping back like a snake if she heard movements below. The blackout was over. Moonlight came in through her bedroom window and wild shapes flailed and gesticulated across the ceiling, whip-lashes, brooms, rearing serpents, racing wolves. When she was very little she had feared them. Now she watched them with delight, and made stories and creatures from them. They were made by the wind in the branches of a wild ash tree that had planted itself, as those trees most tena-ciously do, on the sill of the garden shed.

The thin child's father said it must come down. It was a wild tree, out of place in an urban garden. The child loved the tree, and loved her father, who had been restored to her against all her grim expec-tations. She watched him take an axe to the tree, singing as he hacked, making logs, a stump, bundles of brushwood out of the living wood. A gate closed in her head. She must learn to live in dailiness, she told herself, in a house, in a garden, at home, where there was butter again, and cream, and honey, good to taste. She must savour peace-time.

But on the other side of the closed gate was the bright black world into which she had walked in the time of her evacuation. The World-Ash and the rainbow bridge, seeming everlasting, destroyed in a twinkling of an eye. The wolf with his hackles and bloody teeth, the snake with her crown of fleshy fronds, smiling Loki with fishnet and flames, the horny ship made of dead men's nails, the Fimbulwinter and Surtr's conflagration, the black undifferentiated surface, under a black undifferentiated sky, at the end of things.

ROCKS IN THE RIESENGEBIRGE

THOUGHTS ON MYTHS

Myth comes from 'muthos' in Greek, something said, as opposed to something done. We think of myths as stories, although, as Heather O'Donoghue says in her introduction to her interesting book on the Norse myths, there are myths that are not essentially narratives at all. We think of them loosely as tales which explain, or embody, the origins of our world. Karen Armstrong, in her 'short history of myth', says that myths are ways of making things comprehensible and meaningful in human terms (the sun as a chariot driven by a woman through the firmament) and that they are almost all 'rooted in death and the fear of extinction', Nietzsche, in *The Birth of Tragedy*, sees myths as dreamlike shapes and tales constructed by the Apollonian principle of order and form to protect humans against the apprehension of the Dionysian states of formlessness, chaos and gleeful destruction. Tragedy controls the primeval force of music by presenting us with beautiful illusory forms of gods, demons, men and women, through whom apprehension is bearable and possible. He wrote:

> Every culture that has lost myth has lost, by the same token, its natural healthy creativity. Only a horizon ringed about with myths can unify a culture. The forces of imagination and the Apollonian dream are saved only by myth from indiscriminate rambling. The images of myth must be the daemonic guardians, ubiquitous but unnoticed, presiding over the growth of the child's mind and interpreting to the mature man his life and struggles.

Nietzsche's heroes were Aeschylus and Sophocles whose characters are mythic beings. He did not approve of Euripides, who tried to humanise the actors in these stories, give them individual 'characters' and personalities.

Even as a small child I was aware that there was a difference between reading myths and reading fairy tales, or stories about real people, or stories about imaginary real people. Gods, demons and other actors in myths do not have personalities or characters in the way people in novels do.

They do not have psychology, though Freud used the mythical life of Oedipus as a way of describing the machinery of the unconscious. They have attributes – Hera and Frigg are essentially jealous, Thor is violent, Mars is warlike, Baldur is beautiful and gentle, Diana of Ephesus is fertile and virginal. I remember, seeing that goddess in the stony flesh for the first time, with her many-layered breasts, that I understood there was a sense in which she was more real than I was or would ever be – more people believed in her, thought about her, saw their world in ways dependent on her existence.

Mythical beings are also more and less real than characters in novels. Don Quixote tries to enter the world of myth and the disparity between his real and his imagined worlds becomes almost a mythical force in itself. Anna Karenina, Prince Myshkin, Emma Bovary, Gustav von Aschenbach are human characters with idiosyncrasies and individuality – but their tales are complicated by the presence in them of impersonal myths. Aschenbach is a battleground for Nietzsche's Apollo and Dionysos; Prince Myshkin is a human being trying to be a Christlike man. For several years I used to teach an evening class on Myth and Reality in the

Novel in which we looked at the mythical forms which found themselves as one thread in more (or less) realist fictions. My own novels also have threads of myth in their narrative, which are an essential part of the thought and the form of the books, and of the way the characters take in the world.

I chose the Norse myth of Ragnarök because my childhood experience of reading and rereading *Asgard and the Gods* was the place where I had first experienced the difference between myth and fairy tale. I didn't 'believe in' the Norse gods, and indeed used my sense of their world to come to the conclusion that the Christian story was another myth, the same kind of story about the nature of things, but less interesting and less exciting. The myths didn't give me narrative satisfaction like fairy stories, which seem to me to be stories about stories, to give their reader the pleasure of recognising endlessly repeated variations on the same narrative patterns. In fairy stories – if you accept the bloody violence, and the horrible things that happen to the bad characters – the point is a pleasurable and satisfactory foreseen outcome, where the good survive and multiply and the bad are punished. The Grimms thought their collected fairy tales were the ancient folk religion of their German ancestors but there is a difference. Hans Andersen did not write impersonal fairy stories of this kind, or not often – he wrote nuanced stories with characters, personalities and feelings in them, authored stories, works of the imagination. I felt he was trying to frighten or hurt me as a reader. I still think he was.

Myths are often unsatisfactory, even tormenting. They puzzle and haunt the mind that encounters them. They shape different parts of the world inside our heads, and they shape them not as pleasures, but as encounters with the inapprehensible. The numinous, to use a word that was very fashionable when I was a student. The fairy stories were in my head like little bright necklaces of intricately carved stones and wood and enamels. The myths were cavernous spaces, lit in extreme colours, gloomy, or dazzling, with a kind of cloudy thickness and a kind of overbright transparency about them. I met a description of being taken over by a myth in a poem my mother gave me, W.J. Turner's poem 'Romance'.

RAGNARÖK

When I was but thirteen or so
I went into a golden land,
Chimborazo, Cotopaxi
Took me by the hand.

My father died, my brother too,
They passed like fleeting dreams.
I stood where Popocatapetl
In the sunlight gleams.

I dimly heard the master's voice
And boys far-off at play –
Chimborazo, Cotopaxi
Had stolen me away.

I walked in a great golden dream
To and fro from school –
Shining Popocatapetl
The dusty streets did rule.

I walked home with a gold dark boy,
And never a word I'd say,
Chimborazo, Cotopaxi
Had taken my speech away.

I gazed entranced upon his face
Fairer than any flower –

O shining Popocatapetl
It was thy magic hour:

The houses, people, traffic seemed
Thin fading dreams by day;
Chimborazo, Cotopaxi
They had stolen my soul away!

I recognised that state of mind, that other world. The words in my head were not Chimborazo and Cotopaxi, but Ginnungagap, Yggdrasil and Ragnarök. And in later life there were other moments like this. Aeneas seeing the Sibyl of Cumae writhing in the cave. 'Immanis in antro bacchatur vates.' Or Milton's brilliant Snake crossing Paradise, erect upon his circling folds.

When Canongate invited me to write a myth I knew immediately which myth I wanted to write. It should be Ragnarök, the myth to end all myths, the myth in which the gods themselves were all destroyed. There were versions of this story in which the world, which had ended in a flat plane of black water, was cleansed and resurrected, like the Christian world after the last judgment. But the books I read told me that this could well be a Christian interpolation, and I found it weak and thin compared to all the brilliant destruction. No, the wolf swallowed the king of the gods, the snake poisoned Thor, everything was burned in a red light and drowned in blackness. It was, you might say, satisfactory.

I found it harder than I had expected to find a voice for telling the myth that was not vatic, or chaunting, or admonitory in the wrong way. The civilisation I live in thinks less and less in terms of raw myth, I think, and the idea of many other writers in the Canongate series has been to assimilate the myths into the form of novels, or modern stories, retell the tales as though the people had personalities and psychologies. There is also a particularly interesting retelling of the stories by the Danish novelist Villy Sørensen, published in Danish as *Ragnarok. En gudefortælling* and in English as *The Downfall of the Gods*. Sørensen grew up, he says, in the world influenced by the Christian teaching of N.F.S. Grundtvig, who argued in his *Northern Mythology* (1808) that the war between the Norse gods and the giants was 'the fight of

the spirit against the baser side of human nature
– as culture's perpetual fight against barbarity'.
The followers of Grundtvig believed that the 'new
world' depicted in a poem in the *Elder Edda* as
arising after the catastrophe of Ragnarök – which
was named Gimle – was an analogy of the Christian Second Coming, the new heaven and the new
earth foretold in Revelation. Sørensen suggests, as
did the German scholars who wrote *Asgard and the
Gods*, that because the tales were written down by
Icelanders who were already Christian, their inter-
pretations and forms may have been influenced by
Christianity. The Danes thought in terms of
Ragnarök followed by Gimle after their defeat by
the Prussians in 1864, and Sørensen's version is
part of a Scandinavian attempt to rescue the myth
from the Germanic (and eventually Nazi) connota-
tions involved in the history of Wagner's *Götter-
dämmerung*.

Sørensen's way of rescuing and retelling the
Norse myth is to humanise it as a battlefield
between power and love, with Loki – both god
and giant – as a central and conflicted figure.
Sørensen's Valhalla is human and domestic. His
gods have feelings, doubts, psychological problems.

He ends, not with Gimle, but with the end of the world – he has chosen, he says, between Ragnarök and Gimle, and aroused great anger amongst religious Danes by doing so. What he does, in a very interesting way, is precisely what I felt prohibited from doing.

I tried once or twice to find a way of telling the myth that preserved its distance and difference, and finally realised that I was writing for my childhood self, and the way I had found the myths and thought about the world when I first read *Asgard and the Gods*. So I introduced the figure of the 'thin child in wartime'. This is not a story about this thin child – she is thin partly because she *was* thin, but also because what is described of her world is thin and bright, the inside of her reading and thinking head, and the ways in which she related the worlds of Asgard and *Pilgrim's Progress* to the world and the life she inhabited.

The war might well have destroyed the thin child's world. She built her own contrary myth in her head. Even if – indeed when – she herself came to an end the earth would go on renewing itself. The fair field was full of flowers, the sky was full of birds, the tangled bank hid a world of struggle, water was alive with swimming and wriggling things. The death of the gods is a linear tale, with a beginning, a middle and an end. A human life is a linear tale. Myths proceed to disaster and maybe to resurrection. The thin child believed in the eternal recurrence of growing things, and in weather.

But if you write a version of Ragnarök in the twenty-first century, it is haunted by the imagining of a different end of things. We are a species of animal which is bringing about the end of the world we were born into. Not out of evil or malice, or not mainly, but because of a lopsided mixture of extraordinary cleverness, extraordinary greed, extraordinary proliferation of our own kind, and a biologically built-in short-sightedness. Every day I read of a new extinction, of the bleaching of the coral, and the disappearance of the codfish the thin child caught in the North Sea with a hook and line, when there were always more where those came from. I read of human projects that destroy the world they are in, ingeniously, ambitiously engineered oil wells in deep water, a road across the migration paths of the beasts in the Serengeti park, farming of asparagus in Peru, helium balloons to transport the crops more cheaply, emitting less carbon whilst the farms themselves are dangerously depleting the water that the vegetables, and the humans and other creatures, depend on. I wanted to write the end of our Midgard – but not to write an allegory or a sermon. Almost all the scientists I know think we are bringing about our own extinction, more and more rapidly. The weeds in the fields the thin child sees and thinks of as eternal are many of them already made extinct by modern farming methods. Clouds of plovers do not rise. Thrushes no longer break snails on stones, and the house sparrow has vanished from our gardens. In a way the Midgard Serpent is the central character in my story. She loves to see the fish she kills and consumes, or indeed kills for fun, the coral she crushes and bleaches. She poisons the earth because it is her nature. When I began working on this story I had a metaphor in mind – I saw the death-ship, Naglfar, made of dead men's nails, as an image for what is now known as the trash vortex, the wheeling collection of indestructible plastic in the Pacific, larger than Texas. I thought how it had grown from the plastic beakers Thor Heyerdahl was distressed to find floating in the empty ocean, on his Kon-Tiki voyage in 1947. But I wanted to tell the myth in its own terms, as the thin child discovered it.

I have said I did not want to humanise the gods. But I always had in mind the wisdom of that most intelligent thinker about gods, humans and morality, Ludwig Feuerbach. 'Homo homini deus est', he wrote, describing how our gods of Love, Wrath, Courage, Charity were in fact projections of human qualities we constructed from our sense of ourselves. He was talking about the incarnate god of Christianity, a God in man who to Feuerbach was a man made god. George Eliot translated *The Essence of Christianity* fluently and flexibly, and its influence is strong in her work. But there is a sense in which the Norse Gods are peculiarly human in a different way. They are human because they are limited and stupid. They are greedy and enjoy fighting and playing games. They are cruel and enjoy hunting and jokes. They know Ragnarök is coming but are incapable of imagining any way to fend it off, or change the story. They know how to die gallantly but not how to make a better world. Homo homini lupus est, wrote Hobbes, man is a wolf to man, describing the wolf inside,

Hobbes who had a grim vision of the life of men as solitary, poor, nasty, brutish and short. Loki is the only one who is clever and Loki is irresponsible and wayward and mocking.

Deryck Cooke, in his splendid study of Wagner's Ring Cycle, *I Saw the World End*, shows how intelligently Wagner constructed his character, Loge, from the available sources of the myths. Wagner's Loge is, Cooke says, the god of fire and the god of thought. The Loki of the old myths is only half a god, and possibly related to the giants and demons. It is probably a false etymology that connects the Germanic fire spirit Logi with the Loki of the Eddas, but Wagner's Loge is both a solver of problems and the bringer of the flames that destroy the World-Ash. As a child I had always sympathised with Loki, because he was a clever outsider. When I came to write this tale I realised that Loki was interested in Chaos – his stories contain flames and waterfalls, the formless things inside which chaos theorists perceive order inside disorder. He is interested in the order in destruction and the destruction in order. If I were writing an allegory he would be the detached scientific intelligence which could either save the earth or contribute to its rapid disintegration. As it is, the world ends because neither the all too human gods, with their armies and quarrels, nor the fiery thinker know how to save it.

BIBLIOGRAPHY

The myths

Boyer, Régis, ed. and trans., *L'Edda Poétique*. (Paris: Fayard, 1992) In French; with useful scholarly essays.

Magee, Elizabeth, selec. and ed., *Legends of the Ring*. (London: Folio Society, 2004) This large collection includes translations of parts of the *Prose Edda* by Jean L. Young, and some felicitous translations of *The Mythological Poems of the Elder Edda* by Patricia Terry.

Sturluson, Snorri, *Edda*, ed. and trans. Anthony Faulkes. (London: Everyman, 1987)

Stange, Manfred, ed., *Die Edda*. (Wiesbaden: Marixverlag, 2004) In German; a lively version.

Wägner, W., *Asgard and the Gods*, adap. M.W. Macdowall, and ed. W.S.W. Anson. (London: 1880)

Writings on the myths

Armstrong, Karen, *A Short History of Myth*. (Edinburgh: Canongate Books, 2005)

Boyer, Régis, *Yggdrasill. La réligion des anciens Scandinaves.* (Paris: Bibliothèque historique Payot, 1981, 1992) Authoritative and imaginative.

Cooke, Deryck, *I Saw the World End. A Study of Wagner's Ring.* (London: Clarendon Paperbacks, 1976) This unfortunately posthumously published and uncompleted study of Wagner's operas is full of interesting ideas and information about the myths and Wagner's use of them.

Nietzsche, Friedrich, *The Birth of Tragedy and The Genealogy of Morals*, trans. Francis Golffing. (New York: Anchor Books, 1956) *Die Geburt der Tragödie* was first published in Germany in 1872.

O'Donoghue, Heather, *From Asgard to Valhalla.* (London: I.B. Tauris and Co., 2007) Studies both the myths and later literary uses of them.

Sórensen, Villy, *Ragnarok* (1982), in Danish; trans. Paula Hostrup-Jessen, as *The Downfall of the Gods.* (Lincoln, NE: University of Nebraska Press, 1989)

Steinsland, Gro, *Norrøn Religion.* (Oslo: Pax Forlag, 2005) A beautifully illustrated and interesting study which should be available in English.

Turville-Petre, E.O.G., *Myth and Religion of the North Holt.* (London: Weidenfeld and Nicholson, 1964)

BIBLIOGRAPHY

Some plants and creatures

Ellis, Richard, *Sea Dragons*. (Lawrence, KS: University Press of Kansas, 2003)

Ellis, Richard, *Encyclopedia of the Sea*. (New York: Alfred A. Knopf, 2006)

Gibson, Ray, Benedict Hextall and Alex Rogers, *Photographic Guide to the Sea and Shore Life of Britain and North-West Europe* (Oxford: Oxford University Press, 2001)

Huxley, Anthony, *Plant and Planet*. (London: Allen Lane, 1974); revised edition (London: Pelican, 1978)

Jones, Steve, *Coral: A Pessimist in Paradise*. (New York: Little, Brown, 2007)

Kurlansky, Mark, *Cod*. (New York: Vintage, 1999)

Mech, L. David, *The Wolf: The ecology and behaviour of an endangered species*. (Minneapolis, MN: University of Minnesota Press, 1970, 1981)

Mech, L. David, and Luigi Boitani, eds., *Wolves: Behaviour, Ecology and Conservation*. (Chicago: University of Chicago Press, 2003)

Tudge, Colin, *The Secret Life of Trees: How They Live and Why They Matter*. (London: Penguin, 2006)

Warnings

Ellis, Richard, *The Empty Ocean*. (Washington, DC: Island Press/Shearwater Books, 2003)

Harvey, Graham, *The Killing of the Countryside*. (London: Jonathan Cape, 1997)

Pauly, Daniel, and Jay Maclean, *In a Perfect Ocean: The State of Fisheries and Ecosystems in the North Atlantic Ocean*. (Washington, DC: Island Press, 2003)

Rees, Martin, *Our Final Hour*. (New York: Basic Books, 2003)

Roberts, Callum, *The Unnatural History of the Sea: The Past and Future of Humanity and Fishing*. (London: Octopus, 2007)

And chaos . . .

Gleick, James, *Chaos: Making a New Science*. (New York: Viking Penguin, 1987; and various editions from then on)

Acknowledgements

I should like to thank Jamie Byng for his enthusiasm for this project and Francis Bickmore for editorial wisdom and patience. And I should like to thank Norah Perkins. My friend Jenny Uglow has shared ideas and a passion for the Norse stories. I am particularly indebted to my Danish translator, Claus Bech, who gave me Villy Sørensen's *Ragnarok* in both Danish and English, and shared Danish names for fish. My German translator, Melanie Walz, also helped with German versions of the myths. My agent Deborah Rogers has been wonderfully enthusiastic and helpful, and Mohsen Shah, from Rogers Coleridge and White, has kept everything in more order than seemed possible. My husband, Peter Duffy, as always, listens to problems and excitements, and adds new ideas. My daughter, Miranda Duffy, who once spent time working with wolves, told me what to read, and how wolves behaved.

A NOTE ON THE TYPE

Praised for its clarity, openness and simplicity, Van Dijck is based on the type designed and cut by Christoffel van Dijck in the mid seventeenth century. In 1937, Jan van Krimpen revived van Dijck's typeface for the Monotype Corporation, basing his design on the first edition, from 1671, of Joost van den Vondel's famous translation of Ovid's *Metamorphoses*.